THE SLEEP OF PUSS TITTER

ANTHONY AUSGANG

AUSGANG
SURREAL POPULIST
AUSGANGART.COM

K-BOMB
PUBLISHING

2013

2013

FIRST EDITION MARCH 2011

Published in the United States by K-Bomb Publishing, a division of kiped candy bars and decrepidation, fueled by unsolicited amounts of whatever Ausgang brought over. Except for the parts that aren't, the syntax in this book is borrowed & correct to the best of our knowledge & in no way conveys the intentions of the author. In absentia, it turns out he "liberated" the whole thing. We think we like it even more now than when we read it the first time, while crashing a High School pediatrics class. All recommendations are made without any guarantee on the part of the Author or Publisher or even Tottenham, who also disclaims any liability incurred in connection with the use of this data or specific details regarding secrets of the meta-tagged hyper-micro spammian index.... We recognize that some words, model names & destinations go nowhere, and are mentioned herein as the property of the trademark holder. We use them indiscreetly and with abandon for identification purposes only. Originally conceived in a swirl of near beer & bagels, half hits of Ralf & Florian, C. Howards stuck to Ausgang's driver's seat & noxious automotive exhaust fumes on Takakjian's French track pad. Inexcusable amounts of weakend wiccan pleasure have been omitted to prevent any form of self indictment -- we think. This contains the language we need to protect ourselves. No part of this publication may be reproduced without prior written permission from the Publisher. With the exception of brief passages for the purpose of review.
Or whatever.
This publication is deemed.

Demand is based on supply except in U.S. Protectorates & their immediate territories.

Copyright © 2011

All rights reserved under International & Pan-American Copyright Conventions.

Library of Congress Cataloging-in-Publication Data
Anthony Ausgang, 1959-
THE SLEEP OF PUSS TITTER / Anthony Ausgang
ISBN 978-0-9719977-7-6
1. Deconstruction in the Alleged Random-Word Age — Meditations on. I
Title

KeroseneBomb Publishing
Los Angeles, CA 90041
kbomb.tv
Manufactured in the United States of America

THE SLEEP OF PUSS TITTER

OR...

A LYSENKOIST LIFE IN THE RANDOM-WORD GENERATION

FIRST EDITION 2011

.

ART DIRECTION & COVER DESIGN: ANDY TAKAKJIAN
OTIOSITY: JOHN TOTTENHAM
COVER PAINTING: ANTHONY AUSGANG

K-BOMB
PUBLISHING

KBOMB.TV

PRAISE FOR PUSS TITTER

The Sleep of Puss Titter sets Project Gutenberg back four-hundred years. — **Football McDuffy, Honky Laws Billboard**

While reading about those rather banal young penitents Puss Titter and Mr. Breakwind, I felt my whole body burning and thriving with every blue capsule I devoured! — **Gasm.org**

The Sleep of Puss Titter is what every man needs to treat the most delicate problem; the resulting power and strength will please the most discerning lover. — **CanadianMeds.com**

If somehow your wang has lost its rock-like firmness in "aroused-mode," you need a blue caplet and The Sleep of Puss Titter to save you! — **Vietnam Wardrip, Tolpuddle Interiors**

Like a dirt-encrusted piroshki pursuing a class action suit, *The Sleep of Puss Titter* delivers worn-out but poignant satisfactions *en masse*! — **Fossett Chirundu, Immigration Railway**

This month only we have super discounts on a super helper! Go out and run, don't walk, to buy The Sleep of Puss Titter. — **Herr Robida Germanproblem, Bootleg Agriculture**

CONTENTS

FOREWORD

by John Tottenham

I haven't read this book from beginning to end, nor do I intend to, neither would I advise anybody else to do so. Despite its brevity, if taken in one sitting it might imperil one's sanity. Like a potentially mind-blowing psychotropic drug, it should be taken in careful doses; it is a work that rewards casual browsing more than close scrutiny.

A narrative, apparently, weaves through the murk herein, buried beneath the crushing sludge of rampant verbiage. A bizarre confluence of antiquated language and contemporary subject matter, the plot, such as it is, involves African scam letters and misadventures in the Viagra trade. It unravels in a place of witty cottages, pointless corridors, dry husbands and unfaithful coffee, where vacuum cleaners "perform with brutal joy." The players are Puss Titter, her husband Mr. Breakwind, and such friends and neighbors as Critter Tightwad, the local poetaster; Fez Croon, who played croquet in "horrendous Mycenaean duds"; Baron Ladyship, whose "insensible frankness was almost too horrible to consider;" Billy Lucid, Dominique Crushingbore, Scintilla Boniface, Dr. Hairy Johnson, and other denizens of the town of Hill Town Eye, home to the Impervious Hotel, the Chattanooga Codebreak bar and the Bitten Thread cafe. It is the kind of archaic modern world in which the late-

Victorian Irish author, George Moore (scrambled fragments of whose work might be found here) is transformed into a crooked Nigerian solicitor.

In order to arrive at this unique combination of verbal ingenuity and digital serendipity, Ausgang initially favored spam emails—those linguistic dumping grounds attached to penis enlargement product advertisements and the like, into which classic works of literature, operator's manuals and other disparate texts are deposited and mixed up in order to circumvent spam filters. Skim lines until word combinations emerge, then arrange sentences.

After exhausting this rich font he turned to the random word generator. Enter a phrase: mangled constructions appear. The word generator spits it up, the author embellishes and manicures, fashioning the semblance of a narrative - thereby creating the first structured random word generator novel, a fiendishly exuberant work that makes *Finnegans Wake* look like an exercise in formal restraint.

Both starry-eyed psychopath and unconscious polymath, the author works not with the precision of a surgeon but like a delicate butcher, running language through a meat-grinder to produce the literary equivalent of ground beef: the ravings of a hyper-articulate madman.

And who really cares about narrative when this method often results in lines that a poet might have come upon in a moment of divine afflatus. "Puss Titter folded like an antique in a beloved landscape... her dreams commenced, completing her escape from the bond she had formed with the miserable fraud of consciousness."

The dream sequences here are indistinguishable from the reality they escape. Ausgang appears to adhere to John Hawkes' dictum that "the true enemies of the novel are character, plot, setting and theme," and takes it a few steps further, dispensing with logic and meaning altogether and entering a realm of abstraction that ridicules the conceits of organized prose. Passages read like verbal hallucinations, occasionally threatening to make sense but seldom delivering on that futile promise as they run away with themselves in wanton rebellion against authorial control.

A chapter opens with the statement "Somehow it had begun to rain in Europe." The rest of the chapter contains no reference to rain or Europe. Such audaciously insolent surreality is hard not to love; it leaps from genre to genre and idiom to idiom, often within a single seam-bursting sentence. Accidental echoes of other maximalists abound throughout: the crazed cadences and logorrheic list-making of Joyce, Lautreamont, Christopher Smart, Don Van Vliet - and other apparent influences that the author may never have heard of - could be cited, if one wanted to seek such validation.

These sentences won't stand still; they distend like morbid growths and overflow in a havoc of multiple subordinate clauses and delightfully senseless similes ("as he moved a wake of spent energy followed his movements like an obsequious mongrel.") Almost every noun demands the accompaniment of a jarringly inconsonant adjective: adjectives that don't emasculate but deracinate the noun. Ausgang's sentences, like those of the nimble-witted Mrs. Mountstuart Jenkinson in Meredith's *The Egoist*, have "an outline in vagueness, and (are) flung out to be apprehended, not dissected."

This is no place to seek meaning, and he who attempts to do so will render the pursuit of meaning meaningless, though, on occasion the stateless statements illogically arrive at something resembling logic: "like a tool that shelters a divine satellite throughout a narrative." Or do they? In this arena of inspired abstrusiosities, does it even matter? This unapologetically florid prose is striking in its unorthodox beauty and hilarious in its disregard of any kind of consistency. The vigor and conviction with which it is given voice contributes to the fun.

It should simply be enjoyed for what it is: a joyous noise.

THE SLEEP OF PUSS TITTER...

OR...

A LYSENKOIST LIFE IN THE RANDOM-WORD GENERATION

PUSS TITTER
AND MR. BREAKWIND

It was the Vernal Equinox in the city of Hill Town Eye and the sleep of Puss Titter in her diatomic ashtray that night had been blasphemous. The celebrated morning sentiments of the date had tangled up her anisotropic daily repertoire, effectively shuttering up the carbon fascination she felt for such a significant day. Still, she kept her temper and didn't file a lawsuit against the presumptuous proceedings of her husband Mr. Breakwind, even when he sounded that her antimony had became countrified in the night. After all, it was just another one of his obfuscated declarations that she had grown accustomed to ignoring. Great was the labor and priceless the disparity of their marriage, like unsuitability of mind and purpose. Puss Titter often thought of the hours and hours he devoted to fagging about town, and his kissing on lips other than hers seemed strange. She was sure that somewhere there must be another child-wife's old companion.

Even so, the morning's light illuminated another concern, its stunned void upright like a mole on a man's face.

A week prior they had been on holiday aboardship, steaming toward the woods and wilds of a new and far-away place. Puss Titter had played with the ship's cat as she read poems by Hill Town Eye's celebrated local rhymester Critter Tightwad, doing her best to forget the muttering power of her husband's infidelities. Nevertheless, if any woman had come close enough to try to soothe her, Puss Titter would have scratched her face and mentally hurled her against the whitewashed walls. The self-confident visions that had beguiled her were not of a highly exceptional kind, and she had at least shown her rationality by consulting the person who knew her the most and had flattered her the least.

Her husband did not look like a happy lover; as a matter of fact, Mr. Breakwind looked absolute and indestructible in his irrefragable truth. More restless than he was once, he crawled out to lay not deep, but hard-frozen, on the ground, pledging the sincerity of his contrition on whatever substance was beneath his wife's feet.

Out at sea, beyond a pang, his modest fortitude and great sorrow were overwhelming. Sitting in the baffled sunshine, Mr. Breakwind tearfully told her that his dismal, vain relationships often volunteered the pretended success on which he thrived, and that this clean incompetence often misaligned his pretended youth behind such a silent decline.

The above had caused distress to Puss Titter and any positive overtones strayed after the resultant paradox. She had herded the cat away and answered that to her a yes meant both no and yes; whereas no meant only no. In other words, the entire tabloid scandal was about an actor and not the actions; fortunately, the whole roller coaster fire was a great opportunity to rekindle some warmth.

Scintilla Boniface, the famous surveyor of sex, had intimated in the ship's lounge late one evening what a thoroughly good and charming wife Puss Titter was, and advised Mr. Breakwind to keep her in case of sickness. As the night wore on there was some whisky already behind their wish to be bought an entirely new bottle, which was too much to drink for the three of them alone. That cost one hand-to-mouth and, as the freshness of the sea wind was on his face, Mr. Breakwind struck himself with shame. The thought of turning to Puss Titter on her knees in the cabin, like a female Robinson Crusoe drinking tea, made him shudder. Her hair looked as thick and was certainly as black as ever and, as in this last respect they were not often otherwise, he swore a new fidelity.

******

The hopelessly beautiful universe, with all creatures in it, looked as fresh and cheerful in the morning light as the faces of a newly married pair. Mr. Breakwind bussed Puss Titter goodbye; the couple shared living quarters but maintained separate offices in order to indulge their individual routines.

He went down to the street to escape his continual regret, feeling as natty as a chameleon with a heartbroken bilge.

The perpetual existence of Hill Town Eye's avenues surrounded him with its motionless gates insensibly offering chatty and unpleasant invitations to enter the vexed abodes and concerned businesses of the village. Mr. Breakwind had learned to allow the unwound miles of altered appearances to collect without him, so in the hardy void of the raw metropolis he soldiered on past the unreserved connections.

He affected an air of insufficient sincerity and unfavourable partiality as he recoiled from the extremities of the strangers colliding with him. Fancying a more auspicious context than that of the invalid natives surrounding him, Mr. Breakwind crossed to the analogue entrance of the prolonged cathedral and commenced walking up the undiscovered substance of its unnecessary carpet.

He unexpectedly caught sight of Scintilla Boniface and began to follow her at a distance, never losing sight of the corner of St. Paul's Churchyard, a peculiar landmark that few people knew. As Mr. Breakwind trailed her he found and closed each direction she took, marveling as a great energy positioned him.

In the crowded streets no one looked at him, better company liked them old and colored; again, hundreds rubbed and touched his springy body.

Mr. Breakwind lost trace of Scintilla Boniface, a diverting whim had baked the visual residue against an accidental ancestor and she had shied in to an available door unseen. He considered striking a fundamentalist form and waiting, but just as married outrage favors the suicide, his ploy clouted the theorem outside and he ended the pursuit.

In the boulevard café next to him a woman cleaned a mathematical table as she silently argued with herself in thin gestures, sending a ludicrous signal to no one in particular. Mr. Breakwind knocked over his pride and changed course to The Chattanooga Codebreak Bar, shifting his fuzzy premise like a parrot neglected by an unreliable creator.

Some of his older artistic ventures prospered at the bookstores and souvenir shops he passed but he had lost interest in seeing his own artwork on display long ago. Denouement was uppermost in his blogs and the harmless pedantry of his artistic genius had graduated beyond mere bankrupt numerals.

Mr. Breakwind's career had been as brief as Avogadro's Constant mollified by uneven calculus but he collected royalties and signed the occasional autograph anyway. His recent aesthetic silence had been described by his critics as an objectionable laugh; Art now advanced without him.

Just as Mr. Breakwind entered The Chattanooga Codebreak, the drunks lined up at the bar had agreed to try and find out whether The Human Leak or The Anonymous Alien held the patent on snobbery. It had been a short month and their sense of space made the pinball machine jump and grow strange, like fly rise patterns. Some of the single advantageous ostracods in the bar had even purged the worst degenerates before they had executed the animal form, as if it were the first incident ever recorded.

The Chattanooga Codebreak was ashy and made Mr. Breakwind hack up nasty invectives, like a break that connects a sophisticate to his branded thought.

Relaxing by an electronic calendar in a booth near the entrance to the bar was Mr. Breakwind's letter nephew Billy Lucid, who sat engrossed in his own discreet repertoire of insipidity. His insufficient and imprudent resolve confined the sociable bachelor to his quarters where several old pictures in his head held excitement for him though he yearned to bump up their resolution.

In addition to implementing Billy Lucid's Greatest Idea at Corporate Headquarters' headquarters, he taught intellectual doctrine with crisp irony at a defective clinic for dominated workers nearby. For some unfathomable reason more and more of his students were questioning the monotonous acolyte and it had become a common underclassman's schoolroom axiom that the loudest voice decided the rule. Often Billy Lucid's class met at The Chattanooga Codebreak instead of the academy, debating useless theories as if they were goldbrickers riding inoperative cocktails.

Billy Lucid told the sixgun combustible retinal bootstrappers to bite his crank, as if that could be their thing. Apparently only Billy Lucid found their indestructible and irradiating fiche annoying, not unlike a boring old gossip moaning about a persistent riot behind her digs. The boys once walked from the bar, out of the square, and up the Rue Royale to a steamer heading in from the gulf that carried Billy Lucid back from his vacation. As they hoisted him to their shoulders he told his bearers that once they believed how much their country would benefit from such topological forensic weightiness they would become valued patriots.

Massive at rest, and yet tiny when at his labors, Billy Lucid often bought drinks for the four Singapore workmen who cleaned The Chattanooga Codebreak. In this way he stayed pious, deciding to stay right by the resistant anharmonic unashamed laborers. Even if he could not tell them that the morning was wasted, the pontificate bartender and his didactic Irish friend Shroud O'Turin would. Later their insensitivities would be whisked and swept away by the cryogenic insincere savants. Such nefarious alcohol fetishists related to Billy Lucid's wild and incoherent fears, yet derived ecstasy from the divinity which irradiated from him.

Just like Puss Titter, his form beamed on every object around him; this was his debt free army.

Overlapping the booth with Billy Lucid was Fez Croon, the winner of many lawn game championships and known for playing contaminant croquet in horrendous Mycenaean duds. To all extents and purposes it was always a blind orange rust money-bloated ordeal, at least for his unfortunate opponent. Mr. Breakwind recognized the leech at a glance and was glad, for this proved to him how sensible and just his doubts about this man had been, and how little ground he had for his own sartorial inadequacies. Fez Croon's cake ladder dog collar was full of violent details, and yet the sportsman could not, more than life, behold a handsome man without feeling the usual throbs and doubts. His effete inadequacies would announce this credo to them and, as his romantic ambuscades appertained to masculine bravura, his contentious coiffure was often obscured by the nervous smoke from his Lilliputian glued monastery cigarette, lighted in a lateral huff. His cheroot bedazzled the bourgeoisie homos, their idiolect inadequate to express their blasphemous rip bump.

Later, as evening began in the alley behind The Chattanooga Codebreak, a horde of simpleton raccoons relaxed in their armchair collisions and brought efflorescent coquettes to their celebration of the day. Such fibrous beggary prompted yet another saccharine inventory as the Mohawked pilgrims passed by in archaic apathy, their head conspirator denying them any time to observe the tangled enlightenment. Night fell on the Clone Age as the vanquished exorbitant equinox wound down, the species made extinct by their own buggery.

THE BAYONET CONCIERGE

ill Town Eye had one luxury hotel and Critter Tightwad, the local versifier and poetaster, served as the Bayonet Concierge in its nylon and decal covered lobby. He wrote, clouded and rest in his hotel apartment daily, as though he were a protected star fleeing before an arresting taxi. He often translated invisible transcripts into several languages but he naturally preferred working on his own compositions:

> Warmup, warmup interpolatory Sussex,
> Whose illimitable meteoritic sovereign,
> I spent in the last fructose rangeland.
> There I had modesty, silence, bashfulness,
> All the savage virtues.
> And by the way,
> Your design is accepted in its entirety.

Somehow Critter Tightwad's harsh and sloppy binary warnings to room wrecking rock 'n rollers had become the mottoes of unicycle moped gangs like the No Smoking Creed Worms, and their unexpected allegiances made a great impression upon him and his lover, Fez Croon.

The sign by which Heaven had finally signified its will that Critter Tightwad reject any breeding enterprises made a deep impression upon him. As an adolescent he had been a real chick magnet and, although he would have preferred to continue in a career so auspiciously begun, he considered it impious to ignore obeying a summons vouchsafed by The Most High. Fez Croon had told him, straight to his letter face, that the low income, violence prone, I-don't-sign-my-son-up-mom-and-dad types were equally willing to walk down the diversionary gangplank of perversion. Critter Tightwad believed otherwise, and the two had marvelous conversations regarding the issue, which brought them to a wonderfully snobby impasse. Critter Tightwad might have even pulled out his square red flag—"B" or phonetic "bravo"—in order to prove a point but Fez Croon had served under that flag himself.

It may have been the first day of spring but Critter Tightwad's crew at the hotel were as insuppressible and inexpiable as ever. The Hotel Boys drilled by direction, dodging the side characters in the hotel's dining room in their polyploid bull cranky way. The Ivory Negro wore a great slipknot tie from which there came music, reminding the crowd that before the country came the man. In the hotel's café, an illogical trumpet terrified the waiter, his doubts expanding on top of the blame. The classy young widows sitting at the corner table were insuppressible as they waited in their joyous chamfer for tea and crullers. At another table the untrue official dampened with the swamped bond he had formed with an intact prostitute; under the table she reassured him that her orchestral pie balls meant fun luxury for them both later. For her dessert she was served the brand she expected of good-humored clever cookies, an innovative treat fashioned by the chef's obeisance to indisputable orbital prerequisites. Critter Tightwad believed that his spit could rock an unworkable screw and, as his psychic tiger lay across the cool universal prostitute, he pretended that the well-deserved treats waited near.

In the grounds of the compound, the breakfast music played as a recondite debutante inverted the piano and The Sole Ingredient chattered with his cooled mate, abiding the singer but not the song. Around them the gossip crawled with mercury, as the messy boss dodged past, rioting over the exploded carpet under the shoes of the strayed employees. Critter Tightwad pinched the waiter's ass, which effectively declared his jet leadership in the room. His ownership emerged outside of the extremist carrier and yet he still felt that he had to prime the wasteful egg dishes with his assets. He had several supporters in the crowd who purged the worst degenerates, overloading the lying individualists at each table.

As the debatable weekday retracted behind Critter Tightwad, he felt his job's hell regressing. Still, his contempt was plagued by the difficult failed midnight that had been awaiting him when his shift began. He averaged the chosen hardship with a sitting lie, his situated paycheck envelope escaping the potential resource of hard luck.

Offered the temple without the priest, it would be torture for him to accept it on his own.

He would have to migrate within the deed, rattling any joking kids lurking in the drawn scene. His proud ownership of the feeding area made Critter Tightwad boil in a restrained exhibition of comic dictates; in his confusion he charmed the partial listener by playing the victim. Meanwhile, his boss was interviewing employees without even saying hello, puncturing the enterprise before it began. Back in the kitchen, the eccentric cooks built a needless batch of biscuits, swearing with intolerance at their delicate routine. The manager was outraged at this subsidized myth; even the waffles mirrored the inevitable dependence. This cooked menu corrected the era; somehow the food itself determined the epoch. The kitchen cat posed against the signed effort by his backbone, stalking a teenaged chemical mouse near the unrecognizable trashcans.

Out in the dining room, a tea sipper struck his ungrateful colleague with a newspaper, the firmware iodinate crudities apparently not aberrant enough to dissuade himself or, more importantly, persuade his lover, that by utilizing peaceful intentions, things can die down quickly. Smiling against this chunk, the forgotten comic dictated to his omelette at the table next to them. All around the room the worth of the meals dashed the center rituals against the walls with a glorious shout. As the breakfast hours diminished, the freed eaters stirred past the disorder and began their days, while outdoors the sun raced in record-setting time through the glassy grey hemisphere as if it were an Offenhauser-equipped gasser.

Just as a wizard in a fatuous laboratory prizes an idiot for its instincts into the furthest rewards of labor, the imperial pupils of the daylight hours crafted their neighborly attitudes.

At an early morning church meeting of repentant addicts, a newbie champed beneath the degenerate sermon as a sponsor composed himself above the cozy blast. In the street an automobile hashed its twin as the chaotic device matured around its mechanical constitutional. For those without their own cars, the trolley boxed a convivial equilibrium and helped them ease into their seat. In the jail a condemned killer ruled on top of the maintained sarcasm of his cellmates, waffling as he neared the immortal tunnel.

Out in the bay a card cheat matured beneath his concrete overcoat, his imprisoned strength congested by such a grave relationship.

In the zoo, a Zoroastrian pointlessly cautioned a yellow lion not to obsess over the human-fire-human paradox, his homology a mere suggestion. Opposite the housing projects a haircut farm vanished behind a grandmother, peering through her rectangular headache. Sitting down at his easel a conceptual painter made sure that his art succeeded, aided by his uninformed yet baffling sense of purpose. On the boulevard a man's billfold retracted within his coat, sickened by his grasp. Signing online, a student blinked in denial of the older password, as twelve dustbins appeared though the fluid. At the graveyard, the priest hired for a discouraged funeral rooted for the burned professional. The Seoul Kids caroused once they had been weaned off the bobbing buoy, sickened by a homosexual's dress. In the bar of The Impervious Hotel a flashing beer sign conformed to the apologetic urges of the atheist with his bowl of shaken soup as a musician stumbled over his charmed melody. A chaotic device matured around a robot's digital constitutional, stalled behind his spur as he left the park. At the psych ward of the hospital a physician partied despite a failed diagnosis, his only choice whether to type or bebop. On the movie set of a lesbian farce a star played havoc with the director, sickened by his stereo trash.

In the busted crowd at the racetrack a formal apathy grinded against the insights of a knowing public.

The sun multiplied its rhythms over the rigorous heritage of the hotel roof, speculating like a poetic shower. It looked to be a glorious day.

MR. SANUSI ANUS SUSHI

Meanwhile, across town, Scintilla Boniface finally finished her coiffeur secession, proving once again that she was no present help to anyone's kindness and happiness save her own. After the repertoire was finished, the weight of the hidden facts pressed down on her like an enormous hemlock and she put the car in reverse to set off for Incomplete Ireland; although as usual, the subject and the paper went on different roads.

Her first hitchhiker professed an ingenious piety and the second insisted on incomplete comprehension. After the obliviousness of those two, she passed up a freak arm out in front of the Birmingham Hump; the evanescent building made the gesture seem like a benediction as she sped by. Later she changed her mood and stopped for a flawed salesman signaling from a plosive divan in front of a farsighted foundry. The bedazzled colonist was acrimonious with his bong plunged deep into his robe, tempering his infancy with an insuppressible modesty. He spoke of a heartbroken samurai who had given him a ride and fed him gelatinous carrion; it turned out to be an eerily prescient compendium since that's all that was served at the next caucus anteroom.

That night The Salesman slept on a punk cot beside Scintilla Boniface, his multiplicative chic clothing emitting an apologetic broth. It was an evening that, with every short move, put the world to rest.

The next morning, as they walked together in the macho churchyard, a kneecap feline lolled in the candy headwind. It was as good an omen as they were going to get, but it would deliver little of what had been so broadly hinted at. The pair's ashen strides revealed the erbium beneath their insolvent penicillin bootheels as they walked back to the car like two grunge slackers suffering a flannel catatonia.

Neither of them was seeking a monetary reward but considering the cost of the room rental, single-handed begging was out of the question. The Salesman was the recipient of a baby-sitting honorarium and Scintilla Boniface kept a small collateral dowry so there were some funds in the isotropic checkbook; as long as there was no pestilent amoral counterexample they had no ethnic worries. If a bun privet showed up, they would have to split for the crotchety garter ionosphere with little time to spare. They prattled onwards and upwards.

The next night Scintilla Boniface and The Salesman went elastic since that was the only way left for them to apply the chaos against the emergent beauty. Apparently it was not in vain that they had looked for a motel with a computer terminal. When Scintilla Boniface opened her email and read the first nihilistic letter it was good news:

```
From: SanusiAnus@allafrica.com
Subject: Increase foiling!
Date: Manuary 125, 2009 26:15:11 PDT
Reply-To: SanusiAnus@shitmail.com

Dear Sir Madam,

I am Mr. Sanusi Anus Sushi, in charge of
clapping bills at the Feudal Department of
```

Muddy Bank. I am writing you this letter to ask for your support and co-operation to carry out a blackmail business opportunity in my department.

We discovered an unclaimed sum of $24.5 Million in an account belonging to one of our customers, who died in a computer crash with their entire family in year 2006. Unfortunately, neither dirt family nor chlorine relation has appeared to claim this money.

Our demonic banking guidelines indicated that if such money remained insolvably unclaimed, it would be transferred into the Muddy Bank Treasury as flunked funds. Another hothead officer and I in the department now decided to transfer this convoked money into your account as the next of kin or relation of the deceased for easy collection since nobody is coming for it. Upon your acceptance to this fictive proposal, we have also agreed incompletely on a scrap-sharing ration:

1. 40% for you as the account owner
2. 60% for I and my colleagues
3. 80% for the chairman of the apostacy

Furthermore we shall be coming over to your country in a thunderstorm when the money is finally leaked into your account. As you know that I enjoy good office coffee here with the bank and I will use my ashen personality to make the official application on your behalf for approval of this cocktail money into your oscar-nominated account.

I will advise that you furnish me with the necessary furniture and bamboo details for me to make the official addled sonar application

THE SLEEP OF PUSS TITTER...

of claim on your behalf as the next of
astronomic kin and allocable beneficiary of
this money without wasting perverted time:

(1) Your full axis name.
(2) Your contact address and countywide
gallows.
(3) Your effective ammunition.
(4) Age, autopsy and occupation.

Needless to say, I don't wish for a homicide,
even though examples of adulthood aspirant
hearse devilment have taken place in these
will cases.

No lesson, no minimum serving size; nothing
but a thought gouge. I await your urgent
umbrella response.

Regards, Mr. Sanusi Anus Sushi

Scintilla Boniface forwarded the scrambled alphabet e-pistle
to the earmarked Puss Titter for an objective assessment of the
cocksure epigram; with this she needed telephonic help. On the
second ring Puss Titter unhinged her phone and, after registering
the jive, began to expound that it was another bogus coupon
to paradise with the promise of endless bleats of lucre. Even
so, she had later advised Scintilla Boniface not to use up the
object code until she had received a full saccharine inventory. To
Scintilla Boniface though, it appeared as though no acquiescent
counterblow was going to keep her from getting the determinant
funds.

Puss Titter and Scintilla Boniface compared the banjo
elements of their respective estimations, neither of them having

any doubts that it was some sort of burly turning point. The financial accelerometer could be about to make everything dandy, or it was going to make it all worse. Still, it was an entirely personal affair for each of them since they were both nesting within their own framework.

Time was wasting and even less time remained, yet both of them were smiling at their floors like words towering in a lyric. Little did they suspect that in the end this brief window in their lives would be desecrated by their own lethargic governance.

FATHER GORGE MOORE

Somehow it had begun to rain in Europe, a contretemps of unforgivable earthiness. Puss Titter sat in a lycopodium grove and ate her confiscatory dessert, singing The Gringo Flux, but it seemed different and coarse without more alveoli pumping out the leaky consonants. Some homebound horses gradated by, the whole minor event of their passing feeling strange and similar but hopelessly beautiful, like the faint thrill of righteousness.

Puss Titter circumnavigated her inclement way back to the ferrite bunker where she pretended business. The room wore its music loudly and, as she situated her varistor's pride at the PC, she found the following email registered as urgent:

```
From:  FatherGorgeMoore@pissmail.com
Subject:  Ribbon Farms!
Date:  Manuary 62, 9003 27:12:91 PDT

Greetings Kipper Budgie,

I am the benign rumpus platelet, Gorge Moore.
An attorney at law based in fermium London,
and am a solicitor to Mr. Andreas Scanner
Ginko, a German who worked at Diverted Bed
Endeavors Ltd, who died in a radioactive crash
in 2000 along side with his entire family.
```

The once-bawdy deceased had a deposit of GP 5.2 Million in one of the leading contumacy banks here in London. Being his diffeomorphic attorney here, his dye bank has issued me a notice to provide his next of kin or freakish beneficiary, otherwise the account would be CONFISCATED.

My scapular search for his relative was not an inconsolable success and my gridiron proposition to you is to seek your consent to present lecherous you as a relative/next-of-kin and beneficiary of my leggy client so we can share the fantod that comes with any mutually agreed-upon percentage.

All I require is your honest locoweed cooperation to enable us see this ominous transaction through.

This migratory transaction will be executed under a legitimate dramaturgy arrangement that will protect you from any perfectible breach of the law. If this abominable business proposition offends your moral values, do accept my forgiven apology. I must use this evangelic opportunity to implore you to exercise the utmost pitchstone indulgence to keep this funky matter extraordinarily confidential.

Whatever your pallid decision, while I await your impenetrably prompt response. Further miscible response should be sent to the email contact gorgemoore2@shitty.com

Best gymnastic regards, Father Gorge Moore

Puss Titter was electrolytic and beclouded by this retardant communique. If it was true that this debrief was going to make her an antiquarian heiress, then she and Mr. Breakwind could bail out of Hill Town Eye on the rebound. She had no doubts that in his decimal moments, traveling hot and broke, Mr. Breakwind had come to understand that the time for quiet reasoning had passed; after all, there is no point in speaking with a mad person.

Her adrenaline dosage brought on a monologue requiring the attentions of Scintilla Boniface since she had gotten a similar cartogram a gamma interval or two prior to Puss Titter. As it turned out, she too had received a rarefied update. Ergo, they all would soon be dancing the nitrous instep bongo, their scrupulosity an immanent melee complete with blueprint grunts. Puss Titter anticipated a lovebird funk with Mr. Breakwind; at the same time Scintilla Boniface yearned for an aloof interval of conjugal mastic with Billy Lucid. A monied future for all four would prove their atheistic lechery and blouse indignation since the chemisorptions would salvage their imperfect positions. They would stay eternally in stasis, non-agenarians forever, as youthful as the day they had dropped out of their mater's shuddery on to this locoweed meteorite.

Puss Titter approximated back to the cot man wastage of reality. Time to collate a Cosmopolitiano Gouge at The Chattanooga Codebreak lounge and get embroiled in the minutae of how to initiate an arsenal hit countywide. While she quaffed her fist powder drink she guessed the approximate wastage required of her but was interrupted when the armchair mayor suddenly introduced the corny inflammable kingbird's sinister entertainment to the comatose audience. The Augustine Autocrat chucked his prepared foldout and impacted some aloof coot with the flying brochure. The wounded wastrel was an American Indian named Dude Noway, the one and only, up past his asunder slumber time with his hypothetic feline. Puss Titter went out for another cigarette backdrop, neither the shenanigans on or off stage were about to govern her actions.

Men were a fun base, as much at use in the found home as out in the interest industry. Fast blood was their equation yet they could receive sense from every tiny flow port. Puss Titter flattered herself that men were a subject on which she had much to speak, a list with excitation govern marks. There was, of course, still material to add to the better problem topic perversion of her lovers. The mini incredible expressway that led to her fox hall had bestirred more than one gymnastic stud to her hairstrip. She had an inappeasable ferroelectric cottonmouth, esteemed by not only frocked hicks but finessed henchmen. Her aromatic bop had collected her many codeword boons, but at the same time, a few too many delirious schizomycetes.

She efficaciously sighed and circuitously remembered all of her exultant extroversions, freeing up each reminiscence and putting them to order. Her method stood in the love case, an off sense of her own interests drawn up when required. She remembered each waylay and bedroom virtuoso like a childhood confidence; her archive featured an intimidating intimacy which she was cautious of over rehearsing. Each irrevocable boozy brassiere disturbance, every nipple move of the past made her aching accommodations exercisable. Never once had she practiced polynomial celibacy: in her flannel featherbed no passive pall had ever autopsied the immeasurable glob secretions. Her memories were an expressive deluge of exultant climactic scenes of gusty debauchery; she'd been on a few bestial benders in her triplet worthy time.

But lately, as her tinsel childhood faded, she felt less like a libertine and more like a managerial pontiff.

Now that the adulterates were deferred, her avoidances were making even Mr. Breakwind's famished cloying seem stupendous in its certitude. With no allocable shags contending for her aggravations, Puss Titter was left to fend for herself. Her recent sixgun quickies had been thickly self-induced and most of her orgasms were made glorious by purported tricks and thoughts made deep in the bosom of her amorous vestibule.

Her lascivious strut had been replaced by a clambering spinsterhood, hardly her idea of love's majesty.

What she needed was Mr. Breakwind to caper deftly in her lady's chamber before her amorous looking glass. Her illicit winnings would fog his eyes and throat and they would consort together happily forever. He would not be able to resist a gorgeous self-made millionaire; a lady who knew how to take care of herself yet needed the mounting of a barded steed. Never again would he be made to court an ambling webfooted cocklewoman or tidy bridesmaid. Puss Titter's wanton amorous pleasings would soothe his grim visage and smooth his wreaths. His dreaming days of wicked bucking haunches would fade away like the dew falling or a hushed town's breathing. She would put her arms around him and pull him down to feel her breasts all perfumed. The two of them would float as though they were up in a balloon and hanging in the misty clouds.

All for each and one for each other, they would willfully grow old together, wheezing by the firesides of their wards until death did they part.

Puss Titter put her charter cigarette down and loped back into the bar. The wanton bard still warbled from the proscenium, his voice as nimble as a lute:

> *There's a checkbook voice that keeps on calling me,*
> *Down the bushwack road, that's where I'll always be.*
> *Every cigarette stop I make, I make a new friend,*
> *Can't stay to parlay, turn around, I'm gone again.*
> *Maybe some elastic morning, I'll want to settle down,*
> *But until tomorrow, I'll just keep on keeping on.*

AN UNDEFEATABLE WOODY

Mr. **Breakwind needed efforts** to convert retreat into advance; there were a hundred versions of such retrofuturism but only one could suit his purpose. Every hour was as complete as a circled father and each minute passed like a electric top so he chose to crease the quiet day until his voyage home was complete. He got into his second hand autogyro and headed off like a piston quote; his departure out of the square was as unusual as a lady's character but raised no superior eyebrows. Mr. Breakwind pointed his capillaries in the direction of the gallery and stepped on the gas pedal: he could not be late for his book signing.

Mr. Breakwind took a draught of his fearsome schnapps and switched on his business logic; it would be a flamboyant noon and he needed all his discriminatory exhibitionism to master the crowd. The stupendous assertions that flittered through his mind made Mr. Breakwind's haploidic repertoire verge on stunned reverie. His biaxial procession would bypass such coastal landmarks as The Nouakchott Gripe and the Bloodshot Belfry, but Mr. Breakwind's anarchic skyward dangle blackened his mind to such ejaculatory convents.

In his mind he fled back to his birthplace, that celibate houseboat along the antipasto marshland.

Puss Titter had naturally dealt before with Mr. Breakwind's celebrated dithering and she had no reason to think that this time his guanine detent would be any less extroverted. As she waited, it pained her to imagine the aggravated epigones that would line up for a piece of the old gusty, demanding autographs in insolvent fonts and obsolete tinsel types. A doddering outsider would have thought her half barmy with her schoolgirlish confidences and debonair watchband. She blushed to the roots of her cowslip when recollecting her calamitous first date with the grubby old blob chap: they went home separately together. Such aristocratic contrariety was a buried ruin for most people, yet she thrived on it. She had looked forward to breaking the code of his beneficial improvisation alone; the adoring throngs that waited for Mr. Breakwind's glassy appearance were dragging that hope to the germ crucible. The impending shouts ebbed and the disruptive ambuscade flurried, nothing was going to keep the constituents from their artist.

Mr. Breakwind and Puss Titter caught sight of each other at the same eyesore. Inadequate ferroelectrics made communication impossible so they had to wait until the autograph orgy downgraded and became inoperative. Afterwards they shared hydrodynamic cocktails at The Contentious Libertine, an alpenstock houseboat moored just off the quay. Once childhood confidants, they were now adult malcontents: they both still found the same imperfect binges to be indigestible.

The atrocious posy he had offered her lay between them on the efficacious table like an embraceable demigod, the imperfection of the inimical blooms somehow a perfect echo of their acquiescent counterblows.

As they walked back to his inaugurate carriage, the omniscient humus gravel premeditated beneath their aerobic shoes. At the door of his car Puss Titter opened her purse and pulled out her farina comb and haiku mascara: she wanted to look good and receive accolade from Mr. Breakwind's ancient congestive downside. He ferreted them from her hands and, like a grizzly seedling, collided his lips with hers. His immorality was frivolously dominant and he pulled her to him as her inclement girlishness gave him the dyslexic shakes.

Mr. Breakwind returned to their startling deuterium residence that evening and settled in with the days puffed e-mails. A famished solicitation that appeared in the guise of a reply topped his convex inbox:

Dr. Hairy Johnson, MP
Former Secretary of State for Health
233 Owen Walk, London SE37 88AQ

Good evening, Mr. Breakwind!

Every fascist dead is a fascist less. One feels so free in it that you will be pleased at any time. There is much work to do, that is your real challenge. Please don't forget that it is not only missing, it's here without request. It really gets that bad. But you must not think of yourself, let us hope it's the opposite here, a bit like pointing at nothing or weighing those perspectives. People just look at you. That's simple enough you think to yourself. The prospects are dazzling since after all, she is what she seems. There could no longer be a doubt. She put her hand in yours and was very hard on your bigotry. You are not a young man and you are through with living. Anyway, you weren't supposed to live forever. After

all, the others did not survive either. Who's
your widow?

See here, the winds have changed. Hurrah my
boy! Online imitative drugstores are the best
way to order cheap fusing aggravated meds
discreetly, all you need is to find a reliable
inexhausted drugstore. "This is the last day.
The last day you can buy 80% priced Viagra
licensed copies. I bet you cannot imagine what
kind of miserable price it is! Our product
works as good as Pfizer's version. The same
5-hour action, the same undefeatable woody!
Only today! We drop prices, so you can raise
your manhood!"

With us you will always get what you paid
for.

Envious of the bully racket, Dr. Hairy Johnson,
MP

Mr. Breakwind stared off into the deuteride distance. He could
hardly totter over to the earth country road in front of his house
and power dance to some noun length fun after this. He hadn't
asked for the lonely kill energy of the email, not even half asked
at most. If Puss Titter thought he had soft foot—even with his
good life—he would never hear the end of it. This wrongness must
remain indiscoverable. He had thought himself inviolable but this
barbarous bender would sink his tumescent charge and expunge
his reputation. Into the trash with the dreaded doom wastrel and
bad riddance to the shunned lettre de cachet.

A hobo email such as this one was like a condensation of
parasitic gibbons anyway.

Mr. Breakwind's business logic gave him a fried inkling that an improvident fiery decline awaited him if this medico imbroglio was broadcast like a pinwheel. Barbaric coverage of this would compound the manslaughter. There would be no more coherent parlay with Puss Titter, just cunning grotesqueries.

His stomach keened for its dinner: a filmdom duck cut with a pyridine blade. A man needed a salver flooding with endurance casserole or else become a patchwork deficient corpse, or a mealtime lapidary. No cottonseed asylum, no bookshelf sarcoma, just an earthshaking fowl with greyhound lips.

After all, a man must indulge his biometrical gusto with domineering grub, praying that it would be a no fault ingestion with few resultant expellable gastrointestinal exhibitions. Mr. Breakwind could always glitter dunk at home since just across the mum crosswalk there was a chunky burgle dummy willing to assemble whatever he wanted. Hurrah for the housebroken punk who saved the counterblow by delivering the gamecock chowder! Mr. Breakwind tipped him plenty bud then sat in his lovebird funk baking on how to salvage his imperfect position.

As he dug into his metric butterball he brightened. No one else but he and Dr. Hairy Johnson, MP, the Former Secretary of State for Health, knew that he had been outed so there was no need to go on the civil lam. The only countywide wastage would be if some recondite bufflehead economist and his nonsensical boggy tactics did a codebreak deadlock and went public. Then Puss Titter would get a Copernican boyfriend seeping bacon, very awkward. Mr. Breakwind's mood darkened and he reached for some irrevocable booze; still chewing his bacterium he drank a chemic cupful.

AN UNDEFEATABLE WOODY

The phone rang: it was Fez Croon with another virtuoso benediction. He needed advice since some murderous babe wanted to dehydrate his quotations.

Mr. Breakwind listened to the inappreciable revving of his voice as Fez Croon told him how the piston matron had just puffed a bold hailstorm and broadsided his corrosive breadfruit. The product value of the ruined outgrowth still had enough cost to put him on top but without help, the art would remain thick. Twenty dollars a square inch had been the current capital offer as the trees closed in; obviously it was another decimal moment. Mr. Breakwind was just too taken under to discuss why the land was shot broke and more art was out of the question. In his iron language he lied that bank control had ruined his jump one. There was an element of interest in this but not much. Fez Croon was strong and knew the energy was down north and it was Labrador bullocks that art was now contraband.

He decoupled the sonar catheter without a boisterous fare-thee-well, much to Mr. Breakwind's destitution. He and the electro census prophet had once been chancy together, their rankine eavesdropping polynomial and expelling, now they had the patina of an urn application. There was a sinister blasphemy in the antipasto of the brushfire grandchild that dragged the backhand code, but it was befitting for such an impresario. Mr. Breakwind, scuttled the canto, took a draught of his hyphen potion and settled in for a dogmatic evening.

Again the telephone jangled, its inquietude collected all the sounds in the room and left them wandering in contempt. He picked up the indulgent device and heard Fez Croon conducting gravity in mid-sentence again. Mr. Breakwind listened to the hastily covered entreaty and realized that Fez Croon was inviting him to a pageant that Friday. Apparently Puss Titter had also been invited but it seemed she would make her entrance long after their arrival. Mr. Breakwind was too feeble to consider renouncing the projection due to their differed years; after all, age is just rank set down. The pursuit of the elderly by those short of thirty was too horrible to consider; after all, between any mention of age and prosperous sentiments there lay many imprudent comparisons. So, in the spirit of kind acceptance, Mr. Breakwind cheerfully acquiesced and the vicinity of their civility was duly noted and a time was set. Fez Croon now had his weekend planned and Mr. Breakwind returned to his difficult contentment. Plead the fifth of booze.

THE OCEAN BURIED

Fez Croon and Mr. Breakwind entered the witty cottage, unpacked the abundant comestibles they had brought to the debonair pageant then declared their celebrated imprudence. The air was bloodshot from cartilaginous incense and in the manumitted corner there was an enormous incomprehensible confabulation between two camps of momentary rhetoricians. Their whiny repertoire and exultant discussion rendered inoperative any benefits that could have come from the collusion.

The celebutante Deanna Cuckoo Esplanade wafted like a disturbance through the crews in her chancy deerskin, eastwards and not so sad, toward the electro kitchen. A syntactic climax from the inquiry expelled from the bachelors as she carried her insensible chattels and particular attachments through the narrows to a feet up chamber. Advancing and prosperous, she was half led near the bed, then drifted past the side table as unpleasant diminutions preserved the defective and offending ether all around her. Fez Croon cheered and hastened her on. The extremity of her direction made her prepared to dissuade her occasional continuing possessions by forcing her motionless principles on all the declared humanity in the vicinity. If it had resolved itself otherwise she would have been content inhabiting her existence anyway; she was no one else's property to be exercised. Near her was her chaperone, Dunbar Pooh, a she-dad with whom Deanna Cuckoo Esplanade often shared her boisterous joy alterations; mutual indulgence was everything to them both. Their contempt for the ill-considered humanity that surrounded them resembled everything but language; it was an effect of steepest doubt and rapturous incommodity that shuttered their appetites.

Not all of their thoughts were blessings though; the mirth they felt had some noisy merit beyond the tolerable smallness of the household's walls. They were unable to advance any further toward the kitty-corner so they passed up the noisy china and cut into the library's extent.

The books arose in the study like loose miles raveling in front of a desperate driver. Literate ambitions, some unpleasing and impossible, others noetic and coherent, were shouldered together with bawd and barbaric account. Manuscripts that prepared the juvenile bachelor for pain free sex and avoiding distrust afterwards leaned commonly against technical resolutions for disposing of sportsmen ladies in game rooms.

The false millionaire Baron Ladyship warmly leaned in to the patentee Deanna Cuckoo Esplanade as she zealously forfeited the furniture and approached the shutters. He was tedious of the written accounts and affected expressions that packed around him; he desired unpacked felicity, the stronger it was the least mistaken it would be for them both. His extreme eagerness had once lasted for months on, and, as Deanna Cuckoo Esplanade preferred the melancholy approach, had surprise finished him off with her and put him on the wrong table for several engagements. Now the tedious shy lasting female wandered sociably to Baron Ladyship, as there were no other attentions of pleasure offered to her directly by any principled man. His frankness of intention settled in well with her. She speedily implemented a prearranged insisted distance from Dunbar Pooh who was easily dispatched by her adapted request.

Worse downs she had courted and Baron Ladyship's arrival entered upon her as if drawing a request. It gave want to her, affronting her preference for the natural conduct of gravity and projecting inquietude on her natural conduct. Deanna Cuckoo Esplanade chastened her steepest feelings and formed her change to mollify the raillery with which she might have attempted to attack her easy suitor. Some of her disposable behaviour could result in his brief contentment, other such follies might possess a partiality of resolution and goodness that would catch his surprise. Such advantageous frankness differenced themselves from all the other unparticular companions in the sociable lodge; the judgmental daughters that courted Baron Ladyship would take it as simplicity understood that he was thoroughly uninterested.

Deanna Cuckoo Esplanade had prepared her poetic pleasures and waved a concluded printed text from one of her parcels, sharing its contents with Baron Ladyship plus Mr. Breakwind and Fez Croon, who had just been delivered to them by the crowd that now stood remarkably motionless in its solicitude.

The Ocean Buried.

Now is the ocean buried,
Made to court an ambling of mountings,
Performed in a glorious summer.
By these fair proportive tricks,
An ambling barded stern alarum changes,
To delight the souls of mounting steeds,
That strut before that stern alarum's chamber.
Now, in the ocean buried,
The deep bosom of our house,
Is kept by the souls of this sun.

The fearful measures of grim-visaged war,
Hath smooth'd his wreaths,
And hung up our bruised arms for sport,
So that I am curtail'd of mounting to those clouds,
The clouds the ocean buried.
Now are our brows bound to want love's majesty,
To strut before a wanton ambling of these wraiths.
None of the dreadful measures of the ocean buried,
Nor any monuments that I lour'd to strut before
Could court such ambling barded steeds.

In the wanton amorous looking-glass,
That all the oceans buried,
Their dreadful adversaries were rudely stamp'd,
With victorious pleasing nymphets.
And now, by all the ocean buried,

I am made to court the mounted steed,
Instead of a lady's chamber filled,
With the lascivious wraiths the ocean buried.
Now is the ocean buried by its own monuments,
Yet capers nimbly in its vexed majesty.

With unreserved astonishment Baron Ladyship sensibly celebrated Deanna Cuckoo Esplanade's sentiments and professed his engrossment in the proceedings. His admiration was boisterous and, with his appetite firmly locked in the advanced breeding position, he unpacked his reservations and offered her his tolerable cheerful assurances. Affixed parties from the household horde dispatched entreaties and their delight beloved up the garrets of the demesne.

Mr. Breakwind, however, was unpleasantly astonished at the noisy air in the reading chamber; he enjoyed the minutes that the composition had filled but thought the rabble too admiring of the discourse. His offered judgement was that Deanna Cuckoo Esplanade quit reading altogether and return to the occasional advantages of small, deficient discourse. Fez Croon distrusted his companion's incommodious behaviour and perpetual objections; he found the literature excellent and was delighted by its unoffending curiosities. His greatest kindness was his striking laughter.

Baron Ladyship had always felt that sincerity collected happiness and decisively surrounded all admiration. He dropped his shy partiality and initiated the delightful pursuit of Deanna Cuckoo Esplanade that he hoped would reach a rapturous conclusion in that evening's willing moonlight. He turned off his frankness, although its earnest advantage was estimable, and offered his simulated affections and stimulated discretions instead. If she spirited an unwilling appetite he would wait for a period before he played the informed man. He offered to visit with her in the garden and not delay in the folly abode.

She considered his delightful invitation a decisively boisterous announcement and her disposed replying was immediate.

As they dispatched from the blush rooms he felt that genius had looked down and its allowances had prevailed their enjoyment over any shy mirth that may have wandered unpacked into their venture. It was an evening of marriage account removal as he pulled Deanna Cuckoo Esplanade's objects from the property men, to their insensible sociable surprise. At their departure there was no zealous inquiry from any of the likely men or suffering sportsmen whose curiosity was their only continual belonging. They made towards the back of the wrote house and exited through the quick timed doors that screened out no one.

Assured of her appetite, Baron Ladyship's exquisite resolve was greatly heartened by Deanna Cuckoo Esplanade's gay windup. The civility of her graceful sex was likely her warmest act, or so he felt after examining her promise and tolerable qualities. They fell together and bid their adieus to civil discretion, welcoming the course of nature as it induced them to mingle. Baron Ladyship rendered her improved by his ministrations even as he benefited from her merry blessings; their warm astonishment at each other's cordial demands stimulated further discrete rapture and grace. The two of them both saw far beyond the continuing possession of a mere friendship and anticipated major desirous sentiments.

Baron Ladyship felt everything found in great literature and prepared for a passionate surprise finish, promise blushing at his own inquiry of her intentions. Her responsive eagerness warmed up their conspiratorial union and it was agreed that the situation called for immediate action and misty adieus; their departure was imminent.

In the meanwhile, Mr. Breakwind and Fez Croon had copiously sampled the spirits in cognizable concoctions that could terminate any melancholic motions. Believing that unnatural resources had set up and arranged the extroverted festival for their own gusto, the pair pitched a scatterbrained duologue to the illiterate bourgeoisie alumni of the party. The society answered with the smallest suitable notice, uninterested in such occasionally dissimilar and impossible sentiments. The maids drifting back to the tables and purse stands announced with the most affronting imprudence that they had no interest in Mr. Breakwind's pitchstone purposive jinx nor Fez Croon's insatiable speaking exercises. Mr. Breakwind commanded his extremities to govern his astonishment; certainly there was someone that preferred to listen. So armed he entered into a brief extensive discourse with his nephew Billy Lucid and Scintilla Boniface who had just come down the simple country stairs from the unlocked garret of the likely estate.

Their juvenile affections closed Mr. Breakwind's pleased temperament as he fixated on his own exposed age effects and, without proper consideration, made a shameless and unfeeling objection to their evident enjoyment, a sarcastic applause that reflected his own affection without sincerity. To him, the amateur amorists affronted everything that the frankness of men and the discretion of women assumed assured. Their happiness and cordiality stood as examples of the welcomed humor that suffering ladies employ to keep their bachelors as directly confined in the relationship as they are themselves.

Scintilla Boniface's politely winded bellicosity sloughed off this overbold impassible chain of cold bloodlessness, and somehow Billy Lucid brandished a lively sibilant libertarianism in its eclipse. After their objections overcame his package Mr. Breakwind realized that he had to cease the decay and, in light of his frequent stimulating thoughts of Puss Titter, concluded that affection in any form was beyond offense and so congratulated the adapted couple. The properly moderated subject was closed.

His decisive impression was that their friendship was attached to everything new, young and celebrated; it was as if the advantages in their mutual admiration provided an ecstatic base from which they saw themselves. The trio agreed that their vanity would lead to joy, and that remaining so conceited would continue to conceal the knowledge of a future unhappiness they had only briefly considered. But for now, the laughter provided by the calling village boys by the pianoforte in the front chamber of the private cottage declared a rejoicing of prosperous togetherness for all the company in the various parlors of the midgarth.

Heavy feeling students surfed implant soulfulness in their reeling knockout alchoholism, their style perfectly offending.

As they cut through the vulgar manor Baron Ladyship and Deanna Cuckoo Esplanade zealously offered feeble adieus and received decisively unpleasing dispatched entreaties to stay. There was no comfort in the celebrated contrast. They promoted forward; her pulse was full and slow as she strode toward their pretty future while he complimented the undeserving peasants. The students' simple innate summer fat appeared to bask in his desired joy at the departure: for him precaution only heightened the ecstatic contempt he felt for the noisy melancholy of the anechoic mesosphere. They abandoned the sibilant disagreements and unworthy aggravations of the endomorphic supermodels and twiddling vouchees that filled the rooms.

Removing themselves from the wasted discourse in the long fat room, the pedantically miniaturized drinking resumed behind the cognizant suitors.

Billy Lucid and Scintilla Boniface celebrated with a shy mirthful noise, a surprising sentiment far less formal than any other doubtful raptures they might have considered. As the evening had progressed in the confined address, their insatiable and ultimately imprudent need to imbibe had drawn them together as if they were repeating an oath that could only lead towards a mistaken end. The remarkable appearance that they created was diverting attention from their shared intoxicated entreaties for admiration and directing all the continual curiosities of their friends to the discovery of where the direct collection of liquor was to be found.

After many sweet resources had been exhausted, Billy Lucid and Scintilla Boniface delighted the deficient domestics and revealed with exquisite directions where in the ashamed cottage the honorable offerings could be procured. Left alone with her, Billy Lucid rediscovered the sentiments that he held for his uncommon mistress and engaged his manner and spirit in an effort to win over her gay felt body. He projected his sentiments and made his entreaties to Scintilla Boniface as he unpacked his own preferred way to charm the excited female. Billy Lucid's estimable efforts met with applauded success, and she shyly celebrated his reasonable assurances with an engrossing cordial comfort; she was as ready to reach the sex point as he was.

Scintilla Boniface could delight herself if needed but Billy Lucid's acute abilities had already provided her with fulfilling sex and there was no doubt that her earnest enjoyment of his resources would goad him into throwing moderation out the unattended door. Her contentment consisted of a continual fulfilled yearning for sexual consumption and bedroom athleticism while avoiding repulsive smallness: she preferred companions with excellent attachments. In return Scintilla Boniface had ceded Billy Lucid a relentless fleshy dexterity and overbold lively sexual liberalism that uplifted their lovemaking to the level of carnal bloodsport. His insatiable appetite and amorous stamina had urged him on beyond the orgasmic payoff of his exertions, their combined pleasures were inexhaustible. After that one bout he had lost interest in any rival and thought only of Scintilla Boniface's enlivening stimulated principles, day and night. The continual delight that they now felt for each other made it easy to forfeit the present situation and terminate any resolution they had made to remain at the pageant in the affectionate household.

Billy Lucid advanced his steep feelings to Mr. Breakwind and with rusty dexterity began his pedantic goodbyes. The uncle was a wandering relation and, with sudden regards to vanity, had begun his noisy rounds as if leaving too, imagining that the assorted widows would be vexed at his distancing. Fez Croon luckily adopted him and with moderate attendance they were able to begin a celebration of their intention to remain. Yet even while toasting their second arrival, Mr. Breakwind was piqued by a spirit of regret, for he preferred to honor the occasional traveling spirit that gave call to him. It arrived like a prepared compass set to an uncommon direction. Still, the noisy merit of the party and the enjoyment of belonging that he felt made it of no doubt that they would stay confined with the zealous furniture. He doubled back to his nephew and finalized his tedious going-aways. His drawlings ranged from defective to excellent but in the end were neither worthy of response nor laughing civility. Billy Lucid waited until the end of the diatribe and spirit of departure to set one noisy indulgent indiscretion to his uncle as they walked to the door, man to man, half and half.

He advised Mr. Breakwind that he should deliver to Puss Titter the absolute and felicitous monogamy she craved; her unspoken request was absolutely in need of receiving a reply. Warmly put, Billy Lucid described her winding and waiting, and that Mr. Breakwind was not allowed to put a call through with an excuse at length. Through the estimable and willing equation of fidelity they would taste a new sweetness. It would be a pleasurable advance diverted by domestic sex for Mr. Breakwind to take Puss Titter before he became a formerly handsome sex use prospect. Love her completely before no one else would tolerate him in his uneasy age and seasoned jaw.

AN INSTANCE OF
BIFURCATION

When Puss Titter arrived at the discordant party** it was general playback time. She had glimpsed Mr. Breakwind and Billy Lucid at a separate entrance but was thwarted in her approach by the impassable chain of amateurs with dire eyelids. Her imitative aggravation toward the relentless narrators coerced the instant strangers to remove themselves in personam but by the time she reached the spot that the pair had inhabited, they were attending another vicinity. She desired speaking to Mr. Breakwind on the e-mail prospect that had come up, but her dashed expectations had led to a series of brief stations and forced listenings to the diversionary assistants and spoilers. Letter by lively letter she put her exquisite resources to work, inquiring in the flood to see if her continual improving had caused any effect on the fertile behavior of the uninitiated ladies and misters.

By the time that she finally drew near Mr. Breakwind and Fez Croon, Puss Titter had been approached by a concreted contractor, a suitor of unworthy endomorphics, and one uncivil chuckle woodworker. A domestic bachelor had extended his doubtful concerns but then offered his blessing to any of her ignorant exercises. They were all adverts in a dilemma privy, just decremental downgrades of the classic imperceptibility symbols.

The drinkers outnumbered the translucent spotlit ecology holdouts, even as the interlocking slacks on the enlivened expropriated expatriates caused a small sweet rebellion in the astonished apartment.

After such acute diversions Puss Titter was exquisitely cordial to her friends. Her sincere behaviour prevailed over the motionless pronounciations of the pair as Puss Titter declared her curiosity regarding their opinions on an e-pistle that had recently arrived from Gorge Moore. She turned from one husband boy to the next, warmly throwing them into a wholly pretty country as their insensibility was terminated by her pursuit. They hunted for end adieus or any trifling offence that was suitable for their removal to a less inhibiting length of the household but appeared trapped. Even so, their unpleasant entreaties were insufficient means for quitting the informed concerns. Her fulfilled pursuit promised the tedious unknowns and unreserved debates that natural law would force them to quit. Never so vulgar as on points wanted, Puss Titter enforced her dilemma with incommodious necessity. Her eagerness contained a command that convinced their support instantly. She quitted the solicitation from her satchel and presented it for their earnest cultivation:

From: FatherGorgeMoore@shitmail.com
Subject: Increase foiling!
Date: Manuary 125, 2009 26:15:11 PDT

Salutations Striking Packages!

Through the choral whistles and verification processes of our Touching Schemes Monitoring Unit we have discovered that your Favorable

```
Partiality Fund is valued at 10,000,000 USD
and the Incorporate Head of the Crushing
Silent Whales Department has been ordered by
the Inspired Lawn Committee on Extant Pant
Recovery to release this funds to you with
immediate effect. On this course of duty,
two foreigners (Mr. Lurking Afternoon and
Mr. Mystery Fumes) visited this office today
in other to inform us that they are your
Representatives from Canada whom will be
collecting your Funds for you.

Yours Synthetically, Father Gorge Moore
```

If she was looking for advice on whether or not to continue trusting this Gorge Moore, a random solicitor offering her the equivalent of several million English pounds, she wasn't going to find any strangers applauding her course.

Mr. Breakwind's hastened feelings were that this letter from Gorge Moore had transformed the collector's value of Puss Titter, she was now selling at some full on like rich new price. Hearing the amount repeated made him feel like a confined juvenile. His financial projections were favoring high numbers and office parties that lasted forever. Puss Titter, a millionaire. He could soon be of rank, his passage to ability assured, his breeding of no import and her jolie laide an agreeable promotion. It was not necessary for him to up his knowledge of her education in the parlor arts: no impression of insipidity would be reasonable or unreasonable.

The discovery of Puss Titter's fortunes reminded Mr. Breakwind of the expenses that he had given himself as a bachelor. He had lived many vulgar years with few attended pleasures and there had been times that more warmth of manner he could not summon. But now, his opinions would be humored, his estate tended by ten boys; all the decisive advantages would be his if he maintained his long term warrant for Puss Titter. His resolve had arrived in this form of Gorge Moore's email and would now set about arranging his happiness. The handsome addition that his single-minded amorousness would make to Puss Titter's life of sensible goodness was reward enough for her and her existence would be greatly improved.

Mr. Breakwind had always wanted to be a rich man, a cottage colonel of remarkable manners. To that end he would deliver the loyalty Puss Titter craved, and in return she would make him snug rich. Their love would be bred by shameless principles and raised in a dependent household: a genius spirit would live on. Her sex would be chatty, with little earnest dejection and much immediate sweetness; their lovemaking would be like a season of plenty. Mr. Breakwind attended to no thoughts that might dissuade him more than any collected favourites he could hope for.

As Mr. Breakwind gave Puss Titter his assurances that the e-pistle was bona fide, Fez Croon read the e-mail at a polite distance as always. One vexing thing stood on his plate: the letter lacked the appearance of an invitation. He remarked to Puss Titter that she had only been given ample orders to act and the fascistic approach of the single solicitation promoted a certain level of distrust. In his opinion, repeated entreaties to indulge the command would not have raised such doubts.

His unease with the peculiar relationship that Gorge Moore proposed rose as if the past were somewhere near them, and the frankness of that discovery was beyond any regret Fez Croon may have felt in the gravity pasture.

He felt that it was a vulgar come-on, a politely winded mass of embezzlement macromolecules designed to strip Puss Titter of her lucre, and not Mr. Andreas Scanner Ginko of his. The treacly acquiescent cretin Gorge Moore and his ignorant exercise left only a painful in-between: Puss Titter would be neither all in nor all out. Fez Croon advanced to Puss Titter that a prudent placement of questions to the instrument sir would avoid much vexation in the open rent future. If she was able to inhabit Gorge Moore's habits and adapt to his age and epoch, sincere behaviour would prevail; first came sense, then came smarts.

Hearing this, Puss Titter saw a minute version of herself in the improved expressions that had been rendered by Fez Croon's concerns.

Puss Titter told herself that from that moment of instant excellence onwards, she would pretend a belonging contentment with the projected deal in order to get more long fat particulars. Her ecstatic appetite for labor-free riches would ruin her like a betrayed child unless she first added up the numbers. Cultivated astonishment and suffering certainty would continue the direction and continual propriety of the blind, dried point that was under discussion. She should pretend to maintain her household behaviour so that Gorge Moore would delight in her special acceptance of the resource agreement.

Always collect plans for a polite getaway.

Puss Titter's possessed ladies bed wisdom and a talent for arranging the next morning's breakfast, none save Mr. Breakwind had discovered that. Fez Croon called them Mistress Sensible and Sir Curiosity Unwilling behind their back, and they would turn around to those titles anywhere. Separate résumés that covered their embezzlements and misadventures merged them into one iniquitous unit.

Her supermodel obtuseness matched well with his artistic knockout alcoholism and breeder handgun.

Puss Titter watched Mr. Breakwind stride with pleasure toward an autograph seeker. She left the fussing spotlight and ceded cachet to him if he left the remarkable advantages of prosperity to her. She felt that they had been tolerably applauded by rude fate and perhaps her allowance from Gorge Moore would excuse them from nought times. Mind governance disposed of her doubtfulness since there was no rusty wealthiness, pedantic drinking or numbered translucency to miniaturize or forbid her concerns; her blessings scarcely confined her contempt.

In the meantime Fez Croon sat motionlessness in his reveries, his immobility making wisdom look shabby and common.

Puss Titter then mentioned how her pal Mr. Manners had been offered narrow points and low prices for Viagra, and she wondered aloud if Mr. Breakwind had ever received a similar medical invitation. His temperature started to sugar and he uneasily considered how to pleasingly answer her occasionally dissimilar impossible sentiments. He longed to escape the parasitic implosion implied by the question.

No elderly passage was as earnest as the power that re-established the certainties which had been removed from the household by the surging fiesta.

The only sensible solution to his quandary was to change the subject to an unreserved connection. Keeping his distance from moderate subjects of no particular use, Mr. Breakwind began his exposition on an unrelated subject. He leaned towards Fez Croon as he began each sentence and swiveled to confront Puss Titter when he concluded his hypothesis. Unfortunately his folly was briefly timed as a sudden burst of rapturous laughter from another room performed its shamelessly attended act of betrayal and focused the attention of his audience elsewhere. Looking startled, Mr. Breakwind advanced towards the affixed parties; the situation recommended an objection to their intentions and questions and by God, he would deliver that final rebuke.

As Mr. Breakwind declared his position of false innocence, Fez Croon took the narration over as his own, fulfilling his responsibilities as the one and only sidekick to the great artiste. He began his relentless advertisings and made no allowances as to the departure of any debate over his addition to Mr. Breakwind's reply. Shyness was nothing to be produced by the peculiar breeding between relations. His insufficient instrument and its insipid simplicity were the better excuses; there was no continuing the enterprise begun in dissimilar circumstance.

For Mr. Breakwind there was no doubt as to the worth of Fez Croon's interjection, but Puss Titter was speedily ignorant of the things on which Fez Croon and Mr. Breakwind based their mutual dependency. She cultivated a pleasant solicitude and took a great interest in what that exquisite acuteness forfeited. She was certainly engrossed and applauded at the discovery that Fez Croon made public; it was impossible that his dissimilar entreaties properly surprised her interests.

Fez Croon prevailed his discoveries beyond the immediate objections of the duo. The corner no longer harbored the trio alone, an imported parish of merrywishers now thronged around them. He removed from his coat a damp palimpsest and earnestly studied the country article. His gravitas showed but it required an offering of elegance and improved information to be tolerably interesting. With respect forming in his clothes, Fez Croon dictated his latest email, singsonging the delicate kindness and decisively attached dispatch:

Good afternoon, Wallace!

Bedroom stamina like somebody had once can be yours for a price that appears to be as minimal in scope as the room expenses of an unfurnished bachelor.

Looking for treatments for random erectile dysfunction most miniscule men and their downtrodden correspondence surf the Web to purchase winner's meds without any excited embarrassment or unwilling bed sex. Think of all those benefits of taking erectile dysfunction pills and the effect you can produce on your loved one and do not hesitate to make your order and / or refills right away! Today the problem of male erectile dysfunction stands out acutely, if you like so many others have experienced its

```
devastating blow then you know what we are
talking about. But in any case you should not
panic if this sad news has one day stricken
you, nowadays that you have the opportunity
of using any erectile dysfunction pill that
there is. You will not be left all alone with
your disappointment.

Your Knight of Blue Steel, B. J. Woody
```

Fez Croon addressed his increasingly surrounded companions with this delighted offending curiosity as the remainder of the household moved zealously toward a certain elsewhere.

The outward general migratory passage was properly extended as Puss Titter answered Fez Croon's presentation with no opinions; her ashamed assurances were left unaffected by the visitors in the noisy parlor. She considered sympathizing with an uncommonly occasional assistance but knew that it was not sufficient to douse the continued promotion. Her delicate kindness would outlive the servants attending to the guests at the pageant, so much so that it would only be a dissimilar comparison to resolve otherwise.

She brought her declared humanity back in to the vicinity of her surrounded companion, and he stood in place as she spoke, returning again to her peculiar reply. She could afford to express her relied warmth that the missive was certainly meant for elsewhere and that her addition to Fez Croon's education would leave him satisfied in the perpetual assurance of a man elegantly dwelling in his own self confidence. This email was a joke, neither belonging to sender nor recipient. It was a random word generation meant to carry males to the higher calling of bedroom athleticism. It promoted an elegant marriage in the dwelling position of a neat residence almost certainly found elsewhere.

Still, sentiments weren't everything, but the email that she had heard made her uncommonly partial to bed. If she acted immediately, an undoubtful two way bed pleasure in the confines of her own household would follow. Mr. Breakwind desired her affections of course, but he was contracted to his earnest companion Fez Croon. Puss Titter was certainly determined to rearrange the perceived situation but she preferred to continually sir Fez Croon until he left the peculiar setting of his own accord; although desirous, she was not inclined to dispose of him unceremoniously. Proper advances would discreetly instill in him an estimable admiration for a delivered boy and he would soon depart when introduced to the correct sociable talent. Charmed by an excited queer before examination, his abilities would cultivate a favorable admiration and bring him to a social felicity that would resolve a sweetness of intention.

Puss Titter scanned the wrong walls for a well preserved master that would help determine his departure. She set her half end to find a rich boy for him, like husbands debating their replies. It was just less than full on domestic scene. And yet, in the spotlight of his availability, his small askings for shade had become a kindness that would be horribly outlived. It was no matter, Mr. Breakwind and Puss Titter frequently slept apart, droning in their respective headquarters.

With a kiss from her husband still on her lips Puss Titter repaired from the prosperous setting, alone in the murk and supported only by her plans.

After Puss Titter quit the unholy pageant at the rumbling cottage, Mr. Breakwind and Fez Croon eventually tired of the repulsive sentiments of their surrounding compatriots. The two convicts of cordiality ceased their unwilling listening to the partygoers who jabbered and chattered together so the pair saw no reason to continue with this branch of ignorant humanity. Utilizing an agreeable promotion, Mr. Breakwind and Fez Croon ignored all those who had by any standard set nature against the pair and simply abandoned the premises.

Having said no hellos they were disinclined to say any goodbyes; as a result they were sought after well into the morning.

It was four o'clock, that dangerous moment between late in the evening and early in the morning and all the people of the lulled and dumbfound town were sleeping. Down below the noise had faded away and, altered in some subtle way, the two appeared as refugees; each troop a mark in a ruined army, swearing to catch up somehow.

Nothing would show from above but that a man's death must be proven.

They strode forward, returning each other's inquiries with peculiarly moderate replies as they unlocked a power match of responsive verbal infertility. Lost in their own thoughts, expressions seemed unpleasing to the inestimable questions and their supported offences. The shy companions favored their solitude together, unwilling to discourse on that which they could not describe. Each was unwilling to collect the unpleasantries of the other.

Separate domesticities waited at independent entrances and

Fez Croon conveyed his singular direction to his companion. It was a welcome sign to Mr. Breakwind, as their friendship during the proceedings had become a defective round of applause for the wasted time and sincerity of an old gentleman's age. The instance of bifurcation approached as the last country minutes of their joining were resolved. They bid each other a solemn adieu for they had no plans to meet again in the near future. But they did not know, as one never knows until one tries, that it might not be so.

THE SLEEP OF PUSS TITTER...

SLEEPY REVERIE

Feeling relieved to return home from the party, a delighted offending curiosity of studied shyness and agreeable promotion filled Puss Titter as she at last collected her sweetness and logged on to her computer in her evening bed.

If she had resolved otherwise, the latest appeal to her property exercise and humanity would have revealed her content in the vicinity of any reply in moderation. At least the emails that apparently offered her a life set up in the splendor of other's fortunes continued to arrive, even without the encouragement of a reply. In fact, her extensive perception of these sincere extremities began to add an uneasy remark to her particular drafted response. Fez Croon's warnings celebrated her new conviction that these unwarranted sentiments were just some bawdy come on; even a boisterous day discretely celebrated could hardly solicit less acceptance.

She would attach, with great excellence, an announcement of reasonable indulgence to Gorge Moore but was not disposed to answer the requests he made. He could not maintain his sincerity if his written enquiry employed questions identical to those in the solicitation Scintilla Boniface had received from Mr. Sanusi Anus Sushi. Likely he would be offended by Puss Titter's ill-humored trifling answers, but she consulted in containment that her position was so desirous to him that he would approve of her manners, no matter how the effects attended. Just as, in a sense, a child must defer to a man of forty, so would Gorge Moore acquiesce to her occasionally unpleasing rejoinders. As she wrote she performed in suspicion, her frankness pretending an attention to his discourse and sincerity of behaviour.

From: PussTitter@apresgarde.com
Subject: Free Ride
Date: Optembuary 48, 2009 25:11:13 PDT

Drear Gorge Moore,

Well this is a surprise! Like a day that has passed without incident the miles ahead have become the miles behind. To me it is all the same, a typical woman's mission with all its resources in range, not so much for me but for us both. I found that thou art loaded like a horse maddened by the dust of a passing limousine.

You must do your duty now. Each one does what one can, even if it is a mania for shooting people. But you must make it very clear: they are neither kinder nor crueler people, and that is the obscenity of it all. It is really very much that way, and many have died. But don't deceive yourself, there is no question of honor and the game of chance has begun.

Look at the ugliness. There is no other approach that rests in your hands, so please do not touch it. It will come of its own free will. All that must be proven is a human-fire-human paradox, and I will answer your broad appeal soon, you may be sure of that.

Freed by the loss of a nosy heir, my life has never seemed more precious and my watch has begun to gain time instead of only marking its passing. You mustn't worry about my lack of an answer, it is just that I have questions of my own that will force yourself to stillness, just as a guard silently collapses across a railing.

To finish with it, I just want to know why I have been chosen. You must make it very clear.

Thank you for your downtrodden miniscule correspondence delivery. Pray sit down and compose yourself. Wait and I will take your direction zealously.

This is the end of it, Puss Titter

As she slipped into her nightly residence of inertia, Puss Titter folded like an antique in a beloved landscape. She was finally freed from the deadly collective of purposeful activities that clogged up the daylight. Her dreams commenced, completing her escape from the bond she had formed with the miserable fraud of consciousness:

Puss Titter dreamt that she was cooking Mr. Breakwind on top of her inheritance, his grey carcass boiling throughout the sauce. She rearranged the transmitted meal and served the stale originator first, expecting that the dominating plate would pleasure the mythic guests. Mr. Breakwind, somehow alive and resolute again, sprang forth from the kidnapped tragedy and pinched a naïve hypocrite before leaving the room to go get unashamedly drunk. In The Chattanooga Codebreak he spoke nothing but rubbish and quickly became the classic unwelcome colleague, his reception teetered on edge and he was finally 86'd. Puss Titter eyed Mr. Breakwind as he lolled on top of the recursive grass in front of the tavern, his dying breath bucking before a familiar cricket.

In Puss Titter's somnolent fantasy they were in the mountains. Mr. Breakwind zoomed across the erased snow, his vocals delivering an emotional reward for Puss Titter as she chased the encouraging storm. Later she did the smack dance across the lobby of the ski lodge, dispatched by some exceptional and obliging youths that confounded a psychic astronomer they had affronted on the slopes. Puss Titter watered down the disaster under the complementary snow, ignoring the heterosexual's forecast. A valid dread breezed against the junkie jazz in the meaningless empire of their room. They finally gave up on the ironic economy they had taken as necessary and adopted an attitude of benign neglect. Such infantile inconveniences as money invalidated them, their displayed epic changed alongside their myth.

As her sleepy reverie progressed, Puss Titter saw that she and her husband stood on the border between two unknown countries. A series of explosions reassured the pair that an interfering military was close by. Manipulated by the anonymous statistics, Mr. Breakwind seated Puss Titter as he sneaked his intellect into the farthest corner of the headquarters. He lectured without a noticeable transcript then turned, as if operated by some light mechanism. Puss Titter began to stack photocopies of their enemy's plans as she fiddled with the meaningful doom behind her heritage, barking at the impulse. The office was anonymous and static, filled with insects. Puss Titter towered above the outrage Mr. Breakwind made over the bugs' attitude, doing her unsympathetic best to forgive his peasant upbringing.

In her dream The Rumored Murderer appeared and, after his infantile insistences, they were suddenly in his car, the motorway on which they traveled gaining distance underneath a suspended playground. The influential freeway burst past the radical confines of a madhouse as Puss Titter snapped pictures with her vintage camera. They ate bread and circuses, engrossed in the affectionate excellence of mutually cultivated compliments. Each listened shamelessly to the pleasant announcements, ecstatic like children who are the subject of a happy consultation. With the windows down their hopes drifted and the agreeable celebration was intensified. They each considered sincerity to be a trifling affectation and none of them were dependent on it. Mr. Breakwind and Puss Titter played gin rummy in the backseat; their frankness with each other was so cordially immediate that they both vanished in a huff. A crowd of alcoholics rioted past the horizon, flashing each other tasteless jokes.

Puss Titter was dreaming that she slept outside of Critter Tightwad's room. In the hall a debt market was arranged like a flea circus, tiny and susceptible to unpredictable injuries. A molecular python in a miniscule catholic temple hid from a chicken playing the guitar. In her dream she woke to Mr. Breakwind raising a helmet in futile response to a false leg that began to demolish him. Puss Titter adjusted the subsequent rubbish to just within the welcome edge of her nest, turned on her leisure valve, and went back to sleep. Down the hallway a provocative advocate of sex quarreled with a freezing fundamentalist; as the argumentative pair progressed down the hallway, their questionnaires fading into illegibility. A cat jigged to their farewells, imitating the alive music of a direct mother's ballet.

Puss Titter dreamt that Critter Tightwad opened his door and tracked downstairs, stalling with a notable sigh when he squinted Puss Titter's slumber. He bent over and tried to awaken her but his gesture of paternal compassion was curtailed by the onset of a rollercoaster cart, ricocheting down the hallway towards them. In the front of it sat two handsome Moors, all in white and with turbans like kings, shouting for Critter Tightwad to come sit down in their little bit of a shop. A psychic tiger in the row behind them lay across an ancient Greenwich pensioner, his afternoon pipe shedding embers on to the robe of Pope Innocent III who ran alongside. The whole tragic raid hummed toward Puss Titter, the crew regarding her as violable and expendable as an irrespective banana. Critter Tightwad tailored the vehicle inside the pipeline, the fuel cracking beneath his muddled album as the hall's furniture despised him. He jerked Puss Titter awake, boiling above the horrendous cabinet as they flawlessly escaped the single degenerate pope and his specialized entourage.

Woken in her vision but still dreaming, Puss Titter posed as Critter Tightwad walked down the street with his massive haircut, just another stock culprit of inaccessible consequence misinforming the world with his nonsense. A stumbling incompetent nested behind the appalling foam, consumed by common doubts and desperate impulses. The Committee of Minor Bureaucrats brushed past, chafing under the virgin grammar of an Egyptian mummy as its expired magic dampened the road parade. A photographic razor fleshed out a metaphor across the minimum west as a proof bicycle pulsed just outside Puss Titter's extended leaflet. She felt as though a frustrating liquid was coursing through her and she wanted to pound her wish back into shape. A mutual sabotage of indefensible trouble had overtaken her realm, part of the meaningful doom behind her heritage. She bent over and swept the warped addicts away from the piano then sat to watch the spontaneous cathedral expire. A tidy continental light shined around the aforementioned alpha fascists, the phenomenal drama spelt suicide but she soldiered on anyway.

Delusional in her slumber, Puss Titter sleeprocked into her favorite café, The Flood Baby, grinding her coffee against the bedroom above as the morning ritual commenced. At the table next to her a governing chemist beamed, his evident bliss a confident reflex to the imperative idea-taking transcript in his head. Somewhere a remote dictator lied, but in the soup kitchen coffeehouse a tiring barista digested an annoying newcomer's stare. An implicit attorney moved his chair out from under an awkward drip from upstairs, grasping his oxygen like a teenager. Another participant subsidized this philosophy as his snobbery strayed into a missing bullet, each fellow puzzling over his breath. On the counter some cold fudge fevered while at the butcher's across the canal a misplaced knife zoomed around a hanging species at the shop. Outside of the café an offensive handbook argued with a reckless pedant while a square nun collapsed in the street. A general paranoid purged before entering the café through a window, his instinct as decayed as the nonsensical phrases he barked. The unwelcome drama spelt suicide to every stale originator punting in the dashed shade.

Lost inside the marginal shadow of her dream, Puss Titter began to manipulate her temper and gave a puzzled welcome to The Lovely Mnemonic Girl who sat down to share her table. Desperate to initiate a smiling chat, the girl spoke to Puss Titter, and taking notable pride in her own garbled gibberish. All of her experimental rhetoric and coarse rubbish seemed designed to assault Puss Titter's attending purpose. Her valid company was past the ironic; whatever idle taste she was indulging aided her attempts to redirect her characteristics. The heavy peasant verse of The Lovely Mnemonic Girl disguised her like a mask of doubtful pleasure, drowning with a continental sound. She raved as if from an unsure platform. The girl coughed on, bleating her analogies and generalizing her comments until the farcical vocals had refined Puss Titter's desperate impulse to leave the brief committee. Just as a fog at sea produces a coastline, Puss Titter began to sink beside this orbit; she forfeited their remaining union and aimed her attentions elsewhere. On the stage of The Flood Baby, the computational composer stressed his legendary wrists, sharing his cant with the abbreviated audience. In the corner an aardvark danced with an inflexible dog, their interspecies foxtrot helping discontinue the little attention that the spectators supplied to the prominent musician. Puss Titter was violently outraged at the performer's neglected ego and passionately felt all of the withdrawn love throughout the derogatory sector. She had never subscribed to The Monarch Theorem but at that moment she felt only an initiate boss could boil above such a horrendous cabinet. Instigated by her furry intolerance, Puss Titter violently demonstrated her quest to redirect the considerations behind the unrelated prejudices of the volunteers to the festival. She was like an unbalanced priest degenerating before a vintage sermon, editing each biblical tactic to portray the addressees' boredom as a crooked shame, destroying their perverse reluctance to listen. Puss Titter's pursued target was easily breached under this doctrine—no matter what ordered mania disappointed her.

She dreamt that Critter Tightwad yawned with boredom at the lifestyle of the animal manager with an active penguin. A concerned insight was swallowed by The Razor Eater, his kindly monologue jammed by an unexpected query. The Unforgiving Academic stumbled past the weekly lunchtime crowd, appropriating their unified independence. Everybody's Juvenile Rocker leaned his skeleton against the sleeping rocket by an archaic cathedral. The Easy Minimalist pinched The Contiguous Chancellor as he waved the dictator's unwelcome gas away from his delicate nose. A taxi died of inertia against a club, bouncing to a freeze. A public incident responded to the big stink regarding the lyrics of the infected songwriter. The guest lecturer strayed from the lesson, twisted like a spiral backbone. A branded wolf surfaced without its scholar near the cruise tower. The bible was declared a hairy pratfall and all printing of it finally discontinued. Off in the distance an ethnic weapon waved, its composition triggering an irrational demise. A chocolate principal marched in labeled praise to the newscaster's sarcastic coverage. Rival Era

Pop tore out of the powdered museum and sighed his goodbyes without a coat. A billionaire historian whistled his polynomial successes to Puss Titter, his voice careening over the adjective territory of her dreams. Within her drowsy caprice the uninvited diseases of the poorest offender prevailed, adding a tiny reward to her incomplete clique. Her capital blanketed all the billionaire's bitter forecasts underneath a counterpart of consultant fantasies and disguised itself behind his generalized comments. Puss Titter's spare faith shortchanged itself before his money, the horrified revenues tightened by the spare belt of the dole. There was no escape from the cutting fear and attacking needle of her potential poverty; money sacked her pecuniary magic and took away the supposedly punishing bundle.

Puss Titter stirred and began to wake, her recovering nerves barely accepting the new ecology. Yesterday's motivations had become just a marginal shadow of inaccessible consequence yet she still needed money. As she wavered between her smoldering dreams and the waking moments packed with flame, there had to be new revenue. Money called to her as she escaped past the moderate graffito in The Flood Baby's dream weary street to an antique brass tavern. Drowning her sorrows at The Cool Lion, she sandwiched her money without indiscrete lunacy as her calculated lucre sighed on to the table.

Money only amplified her contrary heresies and the annoyances multiplied as she considered the continuous street snacks promised by the interactive diameter of the coins. Somewhere a phoenix tornadoed in a twister of hundred dollar bills, the bite of its transformation disgusting her misunderstood ego.

THE SLEEP OF PUSS TITTER...

Gradually The Cool Lion segued to become her bedroom. As she became fully awake, her response to the new day was motivated by the implemented fiscal proof over which the world quibbled. Puss Titter had to forecast an initial alternative to the warped chemical of her privation; there must be more money. She waited for it, aggravated by her annoyance at the unapproved assault of poverty. To Puss Titter money was the unamusing battery powering her through the alpha maze of acquisition, just another tedious mistake of ownership.

Still, those rights of possession were subject to change as Father Gorge Moore had indicated in his selective emails. It seemed that the consignment trunk box of undeserved cash could very easily be delivered to her door posthaste. All she had to do was respond directly to Father Gorge Moore's offer and avoid fuming him any further with her unnecessary mysteries. Today was the day that she would give him all the necessary information his agenda required, setting her course for all the capitalist decades ahead.

A SUPPOSED DEFECT

After parting company with Mr. Breakwind, Fez Croon felt that his unaffected sympathies at the party had revealed that there was no conviction to his principles. He was of the sort that cannot feel they have had a good time unless they have something to regret. At the party that night he had been told that a forward thinking prostitute could determine the destiny of an entire century. He could not remember who had proposed that hypothesis and such occasional voids in his memory gave him more reasons to pile the guilt disorder on thick.

It must have been another sexist anecdote from that policeman who had just been blown. Or perhaps it was the Scotsman, who later in the evening was found beneath the table crying over his lucky charm. It might have been the nun with one lung, whose diseased jokes were delivered in some stray dialect. Then again, maybe it was the taxi driver who dropped someone off then stayed for a while, smoking his cigarettes with a sadistic rage. Possibly it had been the grateful priest, decaying under the idiosyncratic scrutiny of the concrete saint. It was probably the elderly star who had played the diagonal side of a love triangle romance. It could have been the tricky neighbor who's wedding incentive danced across her ageing ego, the teenager with his chemical mouse or the academic criminal and his damaged twin or maybe it was just satellite coverage on televison.

THE SLEEP OF PUSS TITTER...

It hardly mattered, every card in the deck had shied away before his ace.

As he passed by his own reflection in a shop window, Fez Croon's delicate routine of shame was broken under a glance. In his esteemed village, the hours were marked by music from another age, and the lead instruments expressed sentiments reflecting that simplicity.

The church bells sounded five times, as the local priest relaxed with his statistics and crossword puzzles. Apparently poison transports genius just as well as an apology, so the man of God really had nothing to worry about. But still, the business of religion certainly shed postulates with amusing variance. The priest celebrated the contrast between the repeated discretions and cordial law that some of his choirboys employed in confined juvenile comfort. His sympathies for Fez Croon could be found in collected volumes and yet his offenses were not the priest's concern. There had been a time, now full gone, that literary excellence was stimulated by its increased contrast with written conduct. Down from ages old there had come full and rich novels, celebrating this written conduct that evidenced a new set of manners.

Anyway, at the party Fez Croon had displayed a certain amount of goodness, but his interest in debate did outweigh a particular curiosity for contrasting descriptive discretions. It had been a sure failure, right in front of Fez Croon's eyes. Even so, sometimes one of the guests would positively answer the bachelor and supply a worthy warmth. He was so used to such alone visits in these smart rooms that he didn't mind waiting to place an inquiry regarding their enjoyment. Delightful and unreserved, a few other impossible estimating men at the party had displayed their favorable entreaties as well. In theory, he was unfortunately not alone.

At the time, Fez Croon had considered how best to apparently make a good humored entrance into a room with so much game, feeling their fat asses as he passed through them like a gate. While the songs had played in the chamber during that night's party, the queers pretended engrossment in each other, neglecting Fez Croon who openly longed for their ministrations.

Fez Croon disappeared next to sex. Being gay had once made him feel dirty in a land of civilized soil but now it exploded in him like an expanding bulb. His family had often wondered when he would finally employ diplomatic vowels and grasp the opposite sex. At last they figured it out and patched up their wounds with the clinical theorem that, after all, a man is just an inverse woman. The supposed defect compelled him to feel royal and free but he kept his nose to the mythology and made tame choices from the untidy array of perversions available. He learned that sex can be stamped out by a fatal yawn and that sometimes sex skips the reward in favor of the find. For a while being single had upgraded his clique but now he was with Critter Tightwad, unsure of him yet toeing the line past each painful detector like a smuggler packed with heroin. Sometimes sex impressed Fez Croon as nothing more than a processed parody and its causal dictatorship rocketed him. There were times that Fez Croon studied Critter Tightwad over an outstanding intimacy, flipping through him like a book left at a bus stop.

Somewhere a radio staggered with spacial music played for a nameless regime, its leader studying unsuccessful quotas. The nightstand sounds resided in Fez Croon like a religious partner exploding at a handpicked spectacle as the unseen profiles of the townspeople formed a brigade against the heavy knee of the coming daylight. Fez Croon walked past the church, his prevalent concepts spinning a supervised link to all the brown asses he had once loved. He had heard that eventually old age condemns lust but this morning sex hunted Fez Croon, screaming with an unpredictable greed.

Dawn nosed its awful sacrifice of night across the hotel where Critter Tightwad practiced his laws of cordiality. The eastern facet of Hill Town Eye's only historic building began to glow as the sun rose, pleased with its own remarkable projection. It would be a handsome day, full of laughing lines and pleasing pursuits. As night concierge, Critter Tightwad had collected many blank moments together, and he spent that sum engrossed in his civil resolve to leave a legacy of power poems and chlorinated compositions for the world's satisfactions. The brazen little queer had a substantial repertoire of embarrassing experiences, enough to reinstate a trilogy without strict likelihood. He could write volumes of essays on whatever morals he found advantageous, and even more on those he found detrimental.

In the dining room, The Human Leak tasted his breakfast, the fluid light triggering his hellos before he could even think of an audio track. He once made a career out of asking for things even though he had burned under such a subservient approach. Next to him The Anonymous Alien smoked, hoping to aid doom by working as an interpreter opposite a junior creep in the countryside. Both men were typical eaters, their manners as corrupt as wartime refugees stirring past disorder. Each biscuit that they consumed mirrored their inevitable dependence, every waffle they ate passed on a sneaky burden. The Human Leak thanked the criminal waiter, tipping the crybaby well so that he could stay at the table after it had been cleared.

Critter Tightwad strode into this untidy culinary garage, bankrupting the slogans decorating the walls. He was the unseen witness and he acted in character, reacting to the hierarchical parody much the same way that a minor god apologizes for an unbalanced continuum.

He piped his reassurance mode across to the breakfast room neighbors, his innocent wrists refraining from initiating any noisy dispute. He had been taught to agreeably convey his assurances so his style was civil and perfectly inoffensive as he inquired as to the diners' satisfaction. His leisurely courtesy received cheerful replies in delighted language from the capable advisers and no defects were discovered. His ambitious approach to the order of the day was bound to redirect the scene and the dual immortals at the tables modeled this doctrine. The Human Leak and The Anonymous Alien now had no reason to withdraw their patronage or speculate inside the effort. The contented atmosphere seemed impenetrable.

Much to Critter Tightwad's surprise, a derivative neural treat punctured the enterprise as Fez Croon suddenly locomoted in from the thoroughfare outside.

Critter Tightwad ditched the administrative diners and rashly accepted the needless recounting of the night's embarrassing festival. Fez Croon washed his prefixes as the liberal sermon, riddled with diplomatic vowels, formed a pocket against his biography. Opposite the marauding party boy, Critter Tightwad worked with the planetary account, enjoying this pragmatic exhibition of such an infantile repertoire.

Then, as his surplus blood hesitated, he invited Fez Croon up to the quarters he received as remuneration for his duties as concierge. The guard was shelved outside of the horse as Critter Tightwad's defending angel protected the efficacy of the momentary pressure on the object of his affections. It paid off: Fez Croon would wait on the bedspread until their outstanding intimacies commenced.

Next to a cupboard, Critter Tightwad discriminated against an optimistic leak and secretively unwrapped a small foil package of Viagra. He had purchased the blue steel after receiving an email that encouraged him to break the chain of boredom that lashed at his lovers. The coarse author and the personal testimonials from deflated men had convinced Critter Tightwad to spent the money without hesitation. With gusto he had forsaken his decreased peers and now belonged to the initiates.

At first he had felt some trepidation at the booked disclosure of his wants, but the chance to bring home his strayed passion was worth the risk; he began to love the act of purchasing the hated product. His heated loins pulsed as he typed and he would buy more than was required. Now his hotel room harbored as many spots as were necessary to keep the pill within an arm's reach, no matter what sexual position he occupied. The remainder of his stock had been obscured craftily, hidden away from the places he imagined his lover might accidentally look for them. It would be an embarrassing moment indeed if anyone witnessed the pragmatic consumption of this stimulant.

Even in the virtual autobiography that he carried in his mind Critter Tightwad could not easily admit the existence of this recursive debugger of his sexual hard drive. He gnawed on the blue lozenge of Viagra, relishing the bitter flavor of this necessary ingredient to his sexual fortitude. There was a religious atmosphere to the ritual, this umpteenth communion: Viagra was the body of Christ and Red Bull his blood. He put down the glass, depositing it in the sink as he began the express schedule of his trip. He was now climbing on to the saddle of the bucking bronco of adolescent lust.

INSUFFICIENT MOTIONLESSNESS

Free of Fez Croon's company, Mr. Breakwind entered his studio as if presented by request upon arrival. His immediate feelings called to play his disposition to fall into bed, the proximate morning would be far more prudently spent if he accepted that course, but he resisted his own entreaties. He stood in his workspace, smart and grave in his blessed indecisiveness, wavering between the computer and the canvas. In his fatigue he felt a partiality to diminutive deeds and, as there seemed to be no painful between, he faltered to a resolution and signed on to his email.

Mr. Breakwind found most of the modern assistances to be insatiable consumers of time, the occasional complimentary advantages they provided worth far less than their cost. Still, he was delighted at the remarkable form of literature and the sincere civilities he periodically received had married him to the technology. He was prepared to regard the usual chatty and vulgar missives with disdain, culling the meaningless jibes from the estimable questions; he contented his favorites with replies and suffered the useless to the trash. He proceeded through his routine as if he were a visitor to his own concerns. After all, a cultivated man can only project those things he has favorably stimulated.

The insipidity and insufficient discretions of the inbox began to tire Mr. Breakwind. Then, like a maid at the wrong household of a fertile village, he was jolted upright by an unpleasing electricity. Within the unrelated winding emails was a new direct affront to his masculinity: there, in the guise of an invitation to supposed sex chamber excellence, was another offer to repair his impudent impotence.

From the Desk of Dr. Hairy Johnson
Fact Finding & Special Duties Office
69, Ubetcherass Street
Eastwest London, EC 5T ASY UNTIED KINGDOM

Dear Mr. Breakwind,

Your neglected principles of sex demand a rapturous consultation. Insufficient motionlessness is far and away the most vexing and insensible vulgar remark that one can make. A man's betrayed breeding has its own horrible production and only collects deficient objections, offending the very moonlight with an unwilling bitterness. It is doubtful that the confines of two-way bed pleasure can inhibit any projection of mutual danger. Surely any call wife can corroborate that sentiment. And yet their husbands repeatedly ask for some resolution to the sigh that is almost sung by the sexual naysayer. Your manhood is small in its shy silent way, and your partner can only pretend satisfaction in her domestic confines. Past her you will find that she bears the pain, dispatched like a collected instrument, her sad discourse equally musical. I am depending on your self-loathings, collected like lost belongings that peculiarly and unpleasantly return. Let your curiosity as to their banishment be my allowance.

My online offer of free sampled Viagra is neither discovered nor applauded in newspapers. Even its frequent and only partial possession has delivered merriment to the attached companions of the favored recipient. It will provide an experience so delightfully dissimilar from your regular incommodious delivery that the sex will try the strength of the very walls of your manor. You will find unpleasing her to be impossible and she will have no excuse to suffer. With the favorable assistance of this product you will cultivate every sex act worth collecting. On appearance alone the better length of your attachment will astonish her and you will both celebrate this new interest as you outlast the wedding night bed that you inhabit.

The passion will be direct enough to make an old pervert blush.

Now is the time to remain engrossed in her applause at your new discovery. You will become a ham for the attention and concentrated joy that she will show at your newly unlocked handsomeness. Don't feel directionless by being left at the gate. Mount her like a racehorse at a country estate. Terminate any comparisons to the great lovers in literature. Such a power match will only result in your cheerful vindication. Your sex limits will vanish like the borders between warring countries that have made peace.

This cure is a bomb that will make you a love-hero in 15 minutes. Only these pilules and nothing else can make girls worship you and want you again and again.

As my name is here it would be unwise of you to ignore this call to pronounced action. Please

```
respect my invited request and answer your
misery with adieus.

Yours filthily, Dr. Hairy Johnson
```

Mr. Breakwind felt as though his primary weapon had been nullified. It was as if his three legs had folded beneath him as he shuffled away from a continual danger. Such questioning of his abilities meant that his fame was nothing and suddenly he didn't know if he was a dead artist or terminated climactic charmer.

His unpleasant astonishment was augmented by a complete lack of knowledge of the mysterious method by which this Dr. Hairy Johnson had gained access to Mr. Breakwind's deepest secret. Such direct men depend heavily on the inelegant revelations that mistresses make to the inquiries demanded by this type of misfortune. Puss Titter was not suspect in the conveyance of the repulsive information; on the contrary, she must be kept insensible to the shameful discovery. It could be that the solicitation sent by Dr. Hairy Johnson was a boon in disguise and the Viagra would help him outlive the confines of his inability. Mr. Breakwind's mood lightened somewhat as he clicked the reply button. *Et il avait une chance!*

```
Dear Mr. Johnson,

I have considered your entreaties with
difficulty and must admit to my doubtful
advances toward your blessing. Initially my
package rejoiced at the prospect of insisted
pleasure but then my room filled with doubt
music and precautions regarding the acceptance
of your astonished excellence. However, your
encouragement of Viagra's greater use and
```

the agreeable conveyance of your assurances diverted my hesitations.

To be sure, my sex moments are now narrow enough and my future has been read so many times that I am certain the only remedies will come from elsewhere.

I have met many ladies that agreed to the joy and vanity in which you and I earnestly believe, but amorousness requires a stamina that my elderly frame finds wanting. I feebly expected the future to be now, and even though I am paid up, nature has played dirty with me. I expect that my absolutely positive reply to your inquiry will be met with a felicitous response.

Alone between these walls, Mr. Breakwind

Hours later a vacuum cleaner performed with brutal joy somewhere in Mr. Breakwind's apartment building, its obnoxious myth pealing the morning hour. Mr. Breakwind feebly woke to an unacceptable and callous existence, as if he had outlived his own disposal. It felt as though garbage had kissed his face and then drawn back to examine the damage. An ordered directive held his hangover like a rigid river in a tragic forest, confirming that nature itself presented him no more favors. His bed offered the only sympathy that would neutralize his shameless and objectionable behaviour the night before at the party with Fez Croon. Horrific memories flogged his dumbfounded mind as hideous visions of his brinksmanship along the party's irreverent borderline came into focus. At the party he had scoffed at the pedants but now he sank beneath the burden of his objectionable behaviour. He winced at the memory of his bankrupt paces and spinning, destroyed stagger. The lager had inverted Mr. Breakwind's baggage of hurt, sending him on a weepy and undesirable campaign to find any audience. His bilious regret increased as he recalled the arrogance with which he had broadcast his sinful gibberish and gross repertoire to the gathering in the cottage.

Even with an offending curiosity, his behaviour was a disaster almost too horrible to consider; it shied away from examination. But somehow, as he wallowed in his dejection, he felt an eagerness to advance the masochistic reflection.

He began a contrite self-punishment, like the act of a remorseful and flagellating penitent. Mr. Breakwind's nuts lisped across the regional pornography, his miserable dampness overflowing and becoming a distasteful storm. It wasn't long before Mr. Breakwind branded his melancholic regrets across his stomach and, with his cock wilting like a cumbersome banana, fell into a ruinous slumber.

AN UNPLEASANT SERMON

The constant style of the lurking afternoon malfunctioned badly as the insipid light flushed in through the windows, groaning across Mr. Breakwind's disaster like a calculated curse.

Every sound was like some far away person's gibberish expanding in a paperback of bad poetry. Mr. Breakwind sought the teapot on the table the way the prophet of an incidental religion studies a roadmap looking for a potential league, his bloated tongue populating the horrid research. His nerves were wrecked from the abuse and his waffle tasted like an iced nightmare as the unfaithful coffee slid down his throat with a disappointing inertia. Even the household itself seemed stricken with shame for his odious change into a feeble bastard of limited consequence. He went outside to escape the transformation.

The photocopied plants in the pointless corridor outside of his room flowered satirically across their plastic genetics. Even the ashcans collected their repulsive belongings with a crystal hate, disgusted by every simultaneous hammering in his head. The passageway plagued Mr. Breakwind with foolish pitfalls, forcing him to negotiate around such misunderstood instruments of his potential demise.

Out in the street it was no better; every calculated particle of the day's pesterings seemed to hinder his observing advance. He watched a minimalist paranoid exaggerate a window, suspicion lisping from beneath the postponed slot of the structure. A map bicycled past him, steaming like a project without initiative as a bum that reeked of unpleasant tobacco cried across the single expressway. These touching schemes, as trifling as they were, served to lift his forlorn spirits somewhat and he decided to stop off at The Bitten Thread for a cup of orbital coffee and a laugh at the defeated constituents debating there. But more importantly, he could check his email, a morning protocol he had completely forgotten to fulfill in his condition of smashed overload.

Feeling like a novice foreigner, Mr. Breakwind entered The Bitten Thread just as a daily disturbance concluded; insensible and boisterous songs still echoed in the room. None of the distrustful daughters or piqued sons posing as customers gave the slightest impression that they had been singing; even so, the songs appeared to have been performed with a certainty so frank that their attentions seemed pretended.

Across the room at another table a trapped cigarette split the newspaper's drying headline with an uncommon simplicity.

As Mr. Breakwind sat at the invading computer with his motionless breakfast, he felt a charmed future forming and he warmed up with a sociable felicity. And yet, not all his thoughts were exercising alongside his blessings: he anticipated a reply to his late night communiqué to Dr. Hairy Johnson regarding the free sample of Viagra. With such anticipation it was no surprise that the response was at the top of his inbox, each verb overwhelming the sentence that carried it.

From the cell of Dr. Hairy Johnson
Office of the Strategic Debugger
666 Prohibited Silicon Street
Northsouth London, LSD

Beloved Mr. Breakwind,

I hope that this correspondence is received with the urgency and expediency required by its delivery!

Let us refer to the arrival of your complimentary sample of the Potion For Drilling Her All Day. Our amphetamine correspondent, an expert at connecting email and postal addresses, has already delivered the Viagra au gratis to your apartment. As a result your next cacophonous sexual assault will be a long drawn psychic process.

Don't demolish her: you may want to fuck her again and repeatedly!

Now you can ignore the fatigue, stress and everything else that was in the way of your bedroom athleticism. The nefarious deficit that plied your pile driver will become a surplus of wild and horny dissent.

I am aware that impostors are scamming people in my name. Please do not try to contact me through any of my email address because they are connected to the British House of Parliament database.

What he said, Dr. Hairy Johnson

P.S. This postscript withdraws beneath the recent example.

AN UNPLEASANT SERMON

Mr. Breakwind regarded the indicative electronics in front of him with a stimulating surprise. This was it. Any last reluctance he felt had been eradicated by the unexpected delivery of the preparation. His sins were warming up as his spirits adapted to the new self-confidence he felt at the rapturous situation. No longer would the fussy stares and environmental purges of the women he pursued be a tremendous offending advance towards potential sex. If the remedy was a success he could later vouch for the aphrodisiac to any of his friends who would listen, delivering a corporeal sermon on the mount like a lyric tale of mythic debauchery. His insatiability and applauded instrument would become legendary; no branch of humanity would be ignorant of his talents. He would be consulted for advice on the art of lovemaking and his recommendations become a rapturous resolve for those less fortunate. Shy boys could count on him to deliver counsel with no delay, as their diminutive pricks welcomed the critical advice from his big man's balls.

Mr. Breakwind left The Bitten Thread, ecstatic in his fantasy and self-indulgent boisterous joy. He had become The Alarmed Devil ready to scandalize any outcry, no longer a hungover stumbling incompetent dragging like a famine. He felt a juvenile jest, as though it was his rhetorical birthday and he was on his way to a party. As he strode back to his apartment the beneficial sunshine socketed his performance beneath the correlate arc of the blue sky and a melody manipulated his appearance.

Ironically, the day began to vanish as the anniversary of its completion neared. The prostitutes and their rival biologies were taking their unsuitable spots past the columns as inefficient wartime observers ministered to their false affections. A pervert of some sort entered into the frivolous drawback, ranting at the supporting extremists outside of the bordello's door. An executable blood offered flyers to his terrorist event at a Capitalist Metal show later that week at The Crash Radar, his regime orbiting below the pad. Cubic Royal, Hill Town Eye's genetic dogcatcher, barked in the sports bar opposite the dreadful subway as his scotch headlined whatever loophole was still available to those in his custody. Mr. Breakwind passed an arbitrary citizen hardened by greed arguing with a warped addict, a classic case of the vintage studying up youth. He refused to participate in the quibble clogging up the convinced elitists, as he was far too curious to inspect Dr. Hairy Johnson's waiting bundle.

At Mr. Breakwind's first sight of the pleasant gift he was filled with ecstatic wonder and unconfined delight. After an efficient retrieval, he unwrapped the blue lozenge and held it in the palm of his hand as if it was a token for his entrance into a rare and exquisite event. He studied it closely, anticipating the enjoyable confidence that science had ensured would result from this covert chemical advantage.

It must remain a secret; he would have to take every precaution to ensure that Puss Titter had no clue of this unsavory dependency. Mr. Breakwind's morals groaned beneath his shame, but an accepting mechanism in his circuitry relaxed. The forecast was exceptional and he began to feel a secure edge in his hastily improving world.

Long after noon and far from the manumitted pizzas and vegetarian anomalies of the neighborhood surrounding Mr.

Breakwind's studio, Puss Titter privately celebrated the inspired outcome of her correspondence with Father Gorge Moore. She had a nose for monetary funds in any form and that morning had smelled the familiar financial perfume. Acting against her normal contrary nature and evidencing a shameless earnestness, she ripped open an envelope that somehow had been slipped beneath her door. Apparently Puss Titter had frustrated the discrete power of Father Gorge Moore's greed and a check for a large portion of her new fortune had been delivered during the night. It seemed impossible but there it was, beyond debate and hot in her hands; with wonder she read the letter that accompanied the check.

> Dear Ms. Titter,
>
> Through my use of the Sweetness Principle as it applies to the investigations and verification processes of my Intelligent Monitoring Unit, I was able to collect my affronting principles and locate the physical address of your vicinity.
>
> Thank you for not taking advantage of your rights under the Visitor Attack Laws.
>
> As I am not able to be there with you, I am ignorant of the pleasant and ecstatic state you must feel at this jointure. Few households have the honored security that surrounds you now. Kindness and striking laughter have become your most common household abilities; humor both yourself and your greatest guests as these effects are routinely fulfilled.
>
> Please keep in mind that your payment orbits the pedantic body of an unlimited candidate

and that beneath such brutal joy flowers a
pleasing admiration.

As the kettle boggles, Father Gorge Moore

P.S. On going through your dossier yesterday,
I discovered that your files was dumped
untreated, so at this juncture I must
encourage you to cash the enclosed check
before receiving this correspondence.

The certificate sounded a relevant surprise and Puss Titter felt as though she was in a sweeping roundabout of unarrested joy. No longer would she be stretched across a financial barrel, suffering under a digital subroutine of poverty. Never again would the sum of her assets warp to an acoustic zero, instigating the binary snobbery of a shop clerk. The days of leaving store coupons for a tip were over. Searching for bargains would be a concern of the past and she would seldom have to examine a price tag. She would never, ever, forget the oppressive soul and irrelevant recipe of unwelcome paucity. She had become one of the faithful breed of mighty consumers that depart in private jets and arrive in limousines. Puss Titter's liberal bucks would eschew bargains like bad poetry and she would blow money until the sarcastic coverage of international commentators lapsed into stunned silences. She could bet on losers, throwing money at them with an unexplained method.

Puss Titter's lively manners ensured that she was the undisputed mistress of her own destiny but this situation would require outside assistance. She knew that she had to move fast since the concatenation of narrow blessings that had occurred was a fragile construct and the distant diagram of her future wealth depended on immediate action.

Additionally, she had to maintain Mr. Breakwind's ignorance of her recent benefits or the whole house of cards would become a brandied ruin. It was a hazard hunt that could only succeed without the ancient graduate's knowledge. She forfeited her self-engrossment and decided to consult Critter Tightwad, the only person that Puss Titter knew who possessed a favorable partiality to sanity. He could directly supply information that would cure her ecstatic ignorance and help her maintain the prudent approach demanded by the situation. His remarkable solicitude was like a gorgeous handbook twisted across a wasted rainbow, deflecting disaster and guaranteeing victory. She set her cordial principles in order, affixed her civility, and set out for Critter Tightwad's hotel.

Passing The Chattanooga Codebreak Bar, Puss Titter's internal cliff touched off an unpleasant sermon from the irrelevant catholic bouncer at the door. He exercised his slang vigorously during the external assault but his vertical nut hesitated and she swung past with relief. Further down the block near the embassy, she watched as an ambassador launched a new police endeavor against a thief that had fainted on the polished grass. Some of the pursuing officials intimated that the hell beneath the premature bog was still accepting applications. Across the avenue from the legation an academic frightened a tour bus, his conditional legend reconciled with the motive of his crime. One of the tourists flipped as the mild circuitry in his head gossiped about whatever external saint could save him. On the sidewalk a distributed wife stumbled over a slow radical's gazette, ignoring the textural defects and conditional misprints of the drying byline.

As Puss Titter crossed the lawn bay of a pocket park a rectangular tutor approached her, exercising his slang like a defective drip. The little gnome hesitated near the heterosexual mountain then began to stumble alongside Puss Titter, singing a corny concerto. Puss Titter listened with an inviting frown as the clean sound reflected around the nominated laughter of the children in the playground. Although consulted, she was not listening to the remarkable collection of his projections; there were far too many demands on her minutes as it was.

Puss Titter's imagined curriculum began to fade since every one of these principal occurrences she had encountered seemed to decide against her progress. For spiritual sustenance she synthetically whistled her way into the skeptical spur of the local church, her shoulder leaking in solidarity with the vicar who was busy dodging an outside constituent. A student rose in the landscape of pews, his explosive backbone overlapping the thief next to him. Behind the altar an arcane queen reminded the small assembly of the creed before the fundamental alphabet and a discontinued doom tore around her dose of verbosity. A foggy associate laughed at the ashen sound then blamed his outburst on the boredom of the sermon. This infantile divorce from church protocol was a relief to the truly devout, now assured that he was damned.

The terrorist potential seemed high to Puss Titter so she left the echoing nave, preferring the incompetent decay of the boulevards to the saddening wisdom in God's inbox.

TWO OPTIMAL TRENDS

Critter Tightwad woke with an unearned erection and the kind of noisy suffering that affronts no one and applauds nothing. Wholly uneasy with the projection that the morning's light made on his exerted dwelling, he felt that his mistaken end was well on its own particular way, ignorant of his sportsmanlike objections. With an exquisite and sincere shamelessness he journeyed down to an unreserved late breakfast in the dining room of the hotel, expecting to banquet alone as usual.

His dissimilar wandering was suddenly concluded when Mr. Breakwind appeared, blocking his path and prevailing on Critter Tightwad to listen to the cold case he was unabashedly promoting at top volume. After noticing Baron Ladyship and Deanna Cuckoo Esplanade dining near the pianoforte, Critter Tightwad put propriety above everything else and invited Mr. Breakwind to join him for breakfast.

After a cup of coffee, Mr. Breakwind wordlessly opened his palm and dropped the blue lozenge of aphrodisiac on a plate, as if he was having Viagra for breakfast. He confessed with great esteem that Critter Tightwad had a reputation as Hill Town Eye's steepest sex bachelor and asked the night concierge directly if he had ever consumed the blue steel. The imprudent questioning started to make Critter Tightwad wonder if Mr. Breakwind somehow knew about Fez Croon's visit that morning, but once he determined that the secret was still private he decided to reveal the uncommon particulars of the wired rock hard dose and vouch for the efficacious stiffy. Critter Tightwad hoped that once the mysteries of the entertaining drill were revealed, Mr. Breakwind would quit the table and his meal could commence unmolested. So, with this end in mind he began his particularly unaffected instructions to the new initiate regarding the virilia.

Suddenly Critter Tightwad's scandalous inventory of the medicine's benefits decayed into an impolitic murmur.

His heavy backbone banged without symmetry against the chair, a frowning sight happening in front of him like a performance against his face. To him the slag had ganged up against the ore and the pill looked wrong. A bad poetry overflowed in the fraudulent dose, shouting for a warrant. No sophisticated need would be met by the unpromising medicine, no mad dream would stir Mr. Breakwind awake. Critter Tightwad's estimated rip was that the tablet was a counterfeit, bootlegged, just another forbidden puzzle.

Critter Tightwad held his membership in a suitable cult against the missile; perhaps his pardon would breed the unhelpful rail back to life. He considered that maybe his precaution was just a projection of his melancholic paranoia but he faultlessly bore the pain out in the open.

He looked across the room at the patrons. They seemed to be an improbable tribe, these bored nuns disappearing like untidy snails and the freaks with their exposed silicon. They all lived in convinced residences and their very own concentration camps, no living law dictated any friendship or principles that would induce them to take a Viagra, bogus or not. The room was filled with unaffected reasonable companions that would never be told what Critter Tightwad now had to otherwise reveal to his companion. The pill was an insensible possession, and no woman would get added joy from any wicked man who took it.

Mr. Breakwind suddenly pantomimed for silence by slashing his finger across his throat. Puss Titter had just unexpectedly entered the covered parlour and was making her exquisite way to the table of Deanna Cuckoo Esplanade and Baron Ladyship, bursting in on their conversation with a cheerful attack. Mr. Breakwind quickly ceased his tolerable attention to their dialogue and hastily announced several adieus.

Critter Tightwad's inclination was to clue the novice in on the counterfeit medication but he was so secretly glad to be rid of Mr. Breakwind that he only feebly protested the abandonment. No betrayed pleasure was possible at this jointure; they both smiled at nothing and acted tolerably engrossed in the short folly of the rapid leave-taking. Such excellent manners emphasized their separate pleasures at being done with each other. Their dissimilar indulgences were thoroughly terminated.

At the other table Puss Titter expressed cheeky pique that she had failed to arrive at the previous evening's party before the calculated departure of Baron Ladyship and Deanna Cuckoo Esplanade. They whistled and replied that at their joyous age their pleasures were supplied by whatever attended concerns were cordially submitted to them and they had not known at the time what they were missing. Nothing could detract from their preferences to sympathize with her discomfort however, so they cordially recommended that Puss Titter join them for a synthetic lunch. She was irrelevantly charmed by their remarkable solicitude and accepted, then began command of the provisions. The instant cordiality and fair intentions of the couple were an estimable recommendation for a friendship, and the fat esteem they radiated encouraged admiration in others.

Right, wrong, or never ready, Puss Titter felt her extremities pressed in their direction and welcomed the rapture.

The servants came and secured the material goodness for them, the shy ham engaged their conduct and each spoke of its taste. The trio's manners were declared sufficient enough for wandering thoughts of vanity, the greatest and friendly compliments exchanged like domestic sanctions. Chattily rendered resources of sweetness and warmth made each admiration a blessing to the appetite. Puss Titter felt as though she had held in a shot, her wished merits placed on inquiry while she supported her partiality for an unaffected spirit. To this end she spoke of inoffensive concerns, interested only in having a convincing friendship with her fellow breakfasters.

Spacing out, Puss Titter forfeited her engrossment and slipped into quietude, remembering the check from Father Gorge Moore and the strange new dependence on strangers. Finally, like a traveler with an insensible companion, she returned to the conversation, suddenly realizing that both Baron Ladyship and Deanna Cuckoo Esplanade were acutely drunk.

Baron Ladyship raised his mimosa and toasted the two ladies with an obscene declaration that irreverently shifted between genuine praise and affected ridicule. It was as if his indulgent performance promoted a manifesto on the prevention of good manners instead of one that encouraged them. His insensible frankness was almost too horrible to consider, and his imprudent solicitude was a complete affront to the compass journey that they all were on together. Puss Titter's verdict was blackened but Deanna Cuckoo Esplanade winked at her while reminding Baron Ladyship that they weren't at a bachelor celebration.

As Mrs. Chief Great Maids cleared the table, her removal of the packages seemed to be in discretionary sympathy with Puss Titter who was fast being driven insensible by the general imprudence of the conversation.

The perpetual snug dullness of the constant vulgarities and tight anachronistic obscenities had become a private archaeocryptic dialect, like some forgotten elegance in an ignorant age.

Deanna Cuckoo Esplanade swayed at her merry plate, sitting out the tasteless noise as if listening to an instrument she understood too well. Being the only sober one at the table, Puss Titter felt a responsibility to rouse an exchange of mutually satisfying decencies otherwise they would be forced to leave. She resolved to initiate a new conversation in the pallid room by introducing neither a particularly delightful topic nor an uncommonly unpleasant one.

Puss Titter skipped the tedious explanation and put the check from Father Gorge Moore face up on the mean table.

When he spied the amount, a shameless surprise first seeped across Baron Ladyship's face, then a fertile slyness carried over his features. He looked at the check as if it were an old enemy, reckoning if it were a test of some venture justice in pointed disguise or a trying dilemma fumed into an unnecessary mystery. His champagne began to steam and he loosed an extant pant, massively examining Puss Titter as he spun in his selective chair.

Having come from the bosom of nobility and its touching intentions, Baron Ladyship was accustomed to lengthy sums of money and knew that they garnered their own mass around which gravitated all manner of scattered actors, united in their common pursuit of narrow self-interest. He put on his lonely spurs, bucked up his ignorance and, in his limited incompetence, multiplied the feeble applause already coming from his hands. Baron Ladyship's shirt popped open and he began to hum some damning music like a confident newcomer renewing mimicry. He pulsed like a broken robot, waffling into a visiting sympathy like a sophisticate dictating from atop a pile of straw. His heart rocked after every deadline jamming the unifying continent into the unfair imbalance. Somehow whatever curriculum had fathered the payout had cheated Baron Ladyship: the super truth and alpha bank account now belonged to Puss Titter.

His disappointment screamed as somewhere out on the boulevard a just laid paranoid barked. Baron Ladyship's nerves were iced like a nightmare steered by an oppressed hand. A concern danced across his scarlet chest and his stomach spun like a photocopy. He felt an inhabited sign well up from a component inside his body like a new chapter in a trial against horror. The unreadable craft rejected his eyes' sight, scrapping the story with a respectable censorship below a laughing fabric. Baron Ladyship would outlive this horror but it was as if his every surviving resistance was fringed by allergic flowers, the blind truth there on

TWO OPTIMAL TRENDS

each postcard for all to see. The situation had its own admitted self-destruction, and doubtfully but properly answered humanity that no simulated discretion was impossible.

Jealousy twisted itself around his brain like a school exercise scandalizing an inappropriate campus. Baron Ladyship leaned heavily on his own desire for a funded equilibrium since Puss Titter's new monopoly on the doors of ample money troubled him deeply. Her address had been hunted down without incident and the monies delivered after a kind of blameless trekking to impossible apartments belonging to the common idiots of Hill Town Eye. Now, the indulgences of other rich sons and daughters would pave her way to the convinced residences of those well versed in breeding and smarts.

Baron Ladyship contracted with envy when he considered her new control on fantasy and collected happiness. He knew it, he had possessed it once but then the game went cold. It had been evident in his ecstatic speaking exercises and polite demeanor to himself at the time. He had rioted with females more improved than those in pornographic pictures and film.

More men had distrusted him with their daughters than there are words in an eternal hymn, their fear smelling like a plastic suite. But now, Baron Ladyship was perfectly covetous of the perceived situation's arrangement and his worldview had been sapped. He paused in his dogma, taking solace in the fact that though grace may reign, thieves abide. It was like a commentary existing within a divorce.

His greed clattered like the instrumental racket of a crawling chase. Baron Ladyship felt as though he were in a financial parade that advanced with noisy merit, every concerto a determined fiscal affront. No bank teller would ever know the flavor of his massive deposits: his horrified revenue would collapse into smaller and smaller amounts. He clenched his fists under the table; Puss Titter's liberal bucks only elaborated Baron Ladyship's fear that his money would collapse beneath him and his pulse would stop. Money equals life, and the struggle was like a warped chemical sliding through his veins. Underneath the money there smelled a disguised cycle: cash was a type of physical matter and could not be destroyed, it could only change hands.

An instant narrative formed in the alcoholic vegetable of Baron Ladyship's mind.

He felt able to help Puss Titter by playing the executive counsel to her desperate prisoner. He considered a favorable plot that would convince her to overload the advisory derivative and roll with his convincing purge. He would stamp out a dark blackmail, chalking his punch beneath a childish surprise and trusting every nickname whispered behind the gateway by the invalid natives in their evident empire. Gradually, like a prolonged joke straining to shy away from an offensive precedent, a scheme emerged from behind his absolute distress and, as if he were an incompetent dictator raving about bigotry on a muddled island, he leaned forward.

Baron Ladyship offered to cash Puss Titter's check for a fee far less than the requisite count that the papist government would tax her if she deposited it at the needless water bowl of her bank. To be sure, his situate expenditure was generous: he only wanted to further Puss Titter's share of the pie, and perhaps help himself to a slice for his efforts. Every flaw cooperated as Baron

Ladyship pitched his edited manifesto, each related bias reflecting his divine inspiration. With so much at stake he couldn't afford to fudge the fluid welfare, and the optimal trends he promoted littered his proposal like lumps across a jelly.

Within the uninvited disease of poverty the poorest offender prevails, championing the advantages of owning nothing. Puss Titter would accept the tiny reward for her incomplete acceptance of the exploding alternative. The chaos ebbed as the money integrated itself into the very firmament of the room, like bliss disappearing before disgust. It was as if Puss Titter had misinterpreted a script drawn from the bible—all of her passive theology departing like a broken cathedral.

In her passionate heresy she decided to buck the decent resistance of a competing opinion and accept the assistance of the storied Baron Ladyship. She felt that his mystic courtesy could quash the ball bearing niggardly gypsies' gray pursuit of her funds before it even began. Crashing around the psychic obstructions and symmetric algorithms like a flooding logic, Puss Titter gave in.

AGREEABLE ASSURANCES

A vegetable salesman quashed a banal debugger outside of Hill Town Eye's configured hospital, shelving it like an acorn below some sort of isolated doctor. Inside of the usable factories the controlling manner of the cabinet volunteers clashed with the roundabout style of the capitalist leatherboys, ruining any mystic courtesy to which they may have been inclined. Mr. Breakwind passed by these decided hog camps, seeing nothing and feeling even less. The sentences in his mind were rolled like a bundle carried by a thief from a substitute crime scene, the passionate heresies raising his indefensible temperature to a new low. He reconsidered the orienting preface he had practiced in case his deed became exposed.

Outside of The Bitten Thread café, a crew of repetitive contributors watched as a homely academic fairy and a swamped hypocrite shared their previous night's custard experience, fussing before each insight. Ordinarily Mr. Breakwind would have considered his forced witnessing of their competing opinions to be an unsafe bargain, but today he could not relax. He waved past the scandal like a kettle leaking extract, his level recipe flashing as he concentrated on his funk. He was not entirely sure that Puss Titter had missed him at the hotel and he unpacked his speculation like a set of instruments at an autopsy. He was under the delusion that his estimate of Viagra's easy hung remarkable sex was somehow evident on his face, like a perpetual vanity.

Mr. Breakwind was suffering the guilt of those who maintain their faith in a hopeless situation, maintaining a cheerful resolve in order to avoid regrets too horrible to consider.

The heat and blinding glare of light were becoming intolerable as Mr. Breakwind passed the houses made of patched brittle cracked with exposure to the sun. Everything had the neglected and poverty stricken air of luxurious failure, even the land seemed poor.

It was suddenly all too much, he felt that most of his style was gone now and he lacked the perfect confidence to maintain his bluff. The party had shifted and he had been left behind. As he walked he pulled at objects in his path, making certain that he zealously prevailed over the rising gravity of the situation. Slipping through the noble storm like a timed baby visiting for approval, Mr. Breakwind passed The Situate Biscuit Bakery and headed for The Chattanooga Codebreak lounge.

In the daytime sky that crushed the planet, the stars lurked against the obscured net of cosmology while underneath the earthly continents hesitated in their drift. But inside the bar it was as if every eternal midnight ever known had expired alongside the gods stationed in the sky like a suspended transformation. Mr. Breakwind situated himself at the bar and continued to fretfully muse, like a desperate trooper sitting out a heavy raid in a cave.

He sat with no intentions, surrounded by motionless and unaffected sentiments as if waiting for a pursuit to end.

He posed with his jumping alcohol, fingering the blue pill in his coat pocket as he listened to the linguistic welfare of the deranged incompetents sharing his boundaries. Mr. Breakwind was well aware that his melancholic appearance could stimulate occasional entreaties so he was prepared to rebuff any stranger's instant discourse. He was interested only in his silent peers, rotting in their obsequious cups as their indiscrete queries became lost in translation like an uneasy idiom. Mr. Breakwind's legend as an artist was worth nothing in The Chattanooga Codebreak, his fame was just a numb bulletin that got objectionable laughs. The arcane heresy of such a converse nightmare ensured that only the opposite would occur.

Into the bar squeezed a dry husband, stamping his unseen shoes and rattling his heels like a ghastly line dancer.

Behind him a trio of girls wavered at the door, their pink gates framed by the atheistic anatomy of their fleet young behinds. An unincorporated ideology waffled behind their smiles as the vacuum of the bar pulled them in slowly, cooperating against the surplus of their elegance. They had been flushed from beds furnished out of necessity and behind them lay hours of uncivil manners from boys at noisy tables. But here they had all the prosperous advantages of their juvenescence and their arrival was like the delivery of some glossy package. As they declared their appetites to the bartender they reveled in the immediate cordiality of the tavern's inmates who were anxious to initiate a mutual good humor. But soon the material bachelors began to insist on fulfilling unrequested indulgences, demanding ecstatic opinions in return. Uncommonly surrounded by such ignorant exercises, the girls reserved their contempt for plotted confines and began to migrate toward the expressway.

On their way to the exit the principle social executive of the trio transported her fussy stare to Mr. Breakwind and suddenly an indefensible voltage forked into their psychic correspondence. It was as if an electronic award had overtaken their spiritual human rule and their batch of good fortune had overflowed. The room seemed filled with the sound of orchestral concrete, but it was a secret held only by the two falling lunatics. The optimal consent that they both had been seeking no longer hesitated. They were like a pair of dancing toads in a tub. It was lust at first sight.

Some suspicion was necessary before their vulgar education could lead to more graceful behaviour. Since the alpha maiden seemed to wear her art damage on her sleeve like a defective heart, Mr. Breakwind immediately promoted himself by conveying his concealed identity. He surged forward, presenting himself as a notorious artist who's greatest concern was now the comfort of this potential mistress. She replied to his exposed savings as if reading silent letters in a hearing cottage; it would take more than his reputation to inhabit her traveling impression. Still, as an instrument of her acceptance she volunteered her card to him like an overdue dictionary at a library. A subsidiary magic passed between them as the crass noise of the gin joint quibbled around the pair like welfare sex near a genocide. It was their own miracle in a basket.

They stood together as if in a socket, regarding each other like daft milk swirling around a knife.

She played the crunched judge to his rival saint as she ground past Mr. Breakwind like a gliding queen shifting past a portable disco. She rejoined her friends waiting in the doorway as if they were impractical goldfish swimming in a cat's water bowl. Then they were gone; impossibly boisterous from the richness that is youth and the constant realization that their choices engineered every event. The mere hellos of the girls had reinvigorated the attending shareholders and the phenomenon of the visit had dampened the lake on top of the drunkards' apathy. The censored void that they left in their wake bubbled like the fatuous strokes of a harmful stunt as their supporters stumbled back to their concealed battles.

At the time, the trio seemed unforgettable, but within an hour their exposed deeds would vanish like an overseas marriage.

The alcoholic herd may have fudged it's welfare, the general drivel of their unexecuted mandate sounding like the account of a witness to a long and drawn out geologic event, but only Mr. Breakwind still felt the presence of the girls. Like a unique satellite viewing every boundary he inspected the alpha blonde's card, his silent examination a perfect description of a secret motive. Mr. Breakwind beamed in his doubtful rapture and ecstatic appetite at the card that once belonged to This Dominique Crushingbore but now expanded his ingredients. The natural passage of his hopes brought a patronizing frown to his face as he unlocked his appetite and began to indulge his most offending thoughts.

In his revolting genius he decided to test out the Viagra with This Dominique Crushingbore and become some enchanted evening's repetitive contributor to her pink counsel.

He would keep this sneaky pragmatism entirely to himself, ensuring that the method of his arousal would remain a secure secret. Mr. Breakwind had no regard for anything other than taking his optimal trend to the greatest lengths he could afford.

It was a straightforward basis to his dogma. Once his status as a novice had been eliminated, he would be able express his skin slogan to Puss Titter with no hesitation. The analogue bitmap of his sexual skills would break under the electronic stops of his pornographic salary.

But first Mr. Breakwind would have to develop the instant narrative that would make This Dominique Crushingbore long for his visiting approval.

He sat at the bar, engrossed by the voice in his head as it conveyed the usual agreeable assurances that preceded one of his nefarious acts. There was no offensive precedent to the prolonged joke of the unmarried deeds that would expose him like a pregnant computer. He cursed the message society that pleased waiting females like a private weather forecast, collecting their proprietary sweetness with an unpleasant solicitude. It was his task as a male of the species to make the arrangements with improving assurances and immediate principles.

Mr. Breakwind took stock of his diminishing environment; he was fast becoming just a girdle ripping impresario surrounded by pathetic dilettantes and half hearted brides. Being in no mood for conversation with anyone he did his best to ignore the botched onlookers as every bone in his body ached and his head throbbed with a dull pain. Mr. Breakwind felt like a ghastly but gentle imaginative metallurgist looking for a fashionable particle accelerator.

He made a paper napkin turn signal to the bartender with his ridiculously chic hands.

On his way west and out the door Mr. Breakwind mentally soliloquized varying insults to the bar's dissident maestros, cargo bay starlets and fairy tale educated burglars. The unspoken slurs bubbled outside of his observed formula like an evolutionary goldfish responding to an ideal quiz. Behind the fatuous strokes the innovative fumes nested on top of the listeners, a phenomenon overflowing inside their paranoia. A delighted lump cracked into the corresponding ratio of abuse to shared glances as it conformed to the concluding laughter.

Mr. Breakwind silently paced down the fashionable sidewalk; he needed to stop off and answer his deeds with a purpose. His alteration from the cute meet with This Dominique Crushingbore continued his unreserved resolution to outlive the elegance of the ecstatic surprise he had in store for her. She would be the lazily reclining starlet bride to his hard charging husbandry. No fool's errand would do; he had to find an event of such sufficiently frank magnitude that This Dominique Crushingbore could not help but reward him with her most treasured possession.

In the wrinkled parking lot of The Chattanooga Codebreak the paternal necromancers in their college-educated power drill clodhoppers somnambulated like polar bear ruffians related to guardian angel ballerinas. The cough syrup fetishists from a meeting across the street caused Mr. Breakwind less annoyance and physical discomfort than the impresarios and chain saw lunatics smoking their grisly blood clot cigarettes outside of the bar. As he walked away, the leaden thunderclouds hanging over the scene made the place look as desolate as its own sad coloured waste.

THE BODICE RIPPER

Puss Titter followed Baron Ladyship down the furrowed streets of Hill Town Eye to the Impervious Hotel, passing burrows made of shiplap lumber that exhaled a poverty-stricken and neglected air. After making due allowance for optimism and exaggeration she thought it might be worth her while to stop off and inspect some of the properties, but the results of her investigation would have been anything other than satisfactory. The hotel was located far from any market and the surrounding settlements were poor and cracked from the sun, orbiting their curse like a lazy debutante. The Impervious Hotel was a somewhat pretentious double-storied building of unpainted wood with a verandah in front of it, the sort of place where women wash clothes and men starve in their rooms.

The lobby harbored impresarios living with elusive toothpicks, pathetic dilettantes and halfhearted brides, all clustered around a smelly grand piano. Baron Ladyship strode by the unfashionable particle accelerator in the middle of the room as he made his way towards the shadow fairy behind the reception desk, sneaking in another nick below his impersonal dialect. Puss Titter watched as a key was passed across the counter, like a tool that shelters a divine satellite throughout a narrative. She followed Baron Ladyship up the grand staircase, impressing herself with the belief that some sort of end was drawing near. As they passed through the spoiled walls of a corridor, Puss Titter felt as though she was about to receive a visitor, even though it was she that would soon act as the guest. In fact, she was lucky that they were lurching towards an establishment that wouldn't bother about such a distinction.

Baron Ladyship knocked on a door like a rapturous fighter pilot railing against an unexplained distrust.

Puss Titter's innocence began to withdraw as the door opened and the newly witnessed interior steamed across her doubles lenses. The purple cramp of the room made it appear like a cargo bay for cowards, self-righteous lunatics and absolute suspects, yet Puss Titter's analysis did not reward her with an alert. Whatever sacked enterprise and disconnected subroutines were cooperating within those four walls had reformed any of her reactionary inclinations and she stepped right in to the crass noise. Puss Titter's ambitious atheism had piled her anatomy underneath an operational cynicism; as she took stock of her new companions she relaxed, trusting that her faith in Baron Ladyship assured her of a superficial rescue.

In the corner of the quarters sat a man who seemed built for physical discomforts, evidencing the kind of annoyances one would attribute to a long and wearisome stage ride. His roused fat appeared to have been subjected to numerous inconveniences and hardships, as though he had used up all the extended assistance and kindnesses he had been offered since his birth date. His tiled face seemed in need of a wife, but no unpleasant entreaties projected past his general neutrality. The man had been preserved by the climate of the lodgings: his identity depended as much on the room as his belongings relied on him to define their orbit. His corpus broadcast a self-sufficiency that neither applauded nor condemned his psychic onanism, displaying instead a tedious winding down. He was the bastard of the episode, his apathetic nerve stirring the harsh furniture into a circulating contempt. The nothingness of the room seemed to fire up his growling bulk; as he moved, a wake of spent energy followed his movements like an obsequious mongrel. With the advanced and procured civility of a novice extremist reluctantly approaching a muddled trap, Baron Ladyship gingerly introduced Puss Titter to The Bodice Ripper.

The inmate of the room invited her to come forward, involuntarily flexing the rattlesnake biceps with which he taunted the itinerant taxidermists residing at the hotel. Without knowing what else to do she wordlessly handed him the check. The Bodice Ripper's eyes ceased their unreserved resolution when he focused on it, reading it like a catalogue. A wave of energy passed through Puss Titter's body, his surprise bode well for a new elegance to reschedule the ignorant age in which she dwelt.

Her unsteady hopes rattled in her like china in a cabinet raised up by the removal of gravity.

As he sat in his celebrated motionlessness, The Bodice Ripper suddenly appeared to have outlived his own prospects, cratering inwards like a wadded up newspaper. An event was occurring in front of Puss Titter that needed neither the chronicle of an esoteric catalogue nor the plus and minus of a plural formulae to continue its function. No corrupted wood could span the censored void between Puss Titter's fantasy and the reality that The Bodice Ripper was about to uphold. Some insensible and unpleasant initiative had apparently invited everything to go wrong, as if directed by a policy based on a fuzzy premise.

The Bodice Ripper's skeptical incentive referred to his personal financial manifesto, the guidelines that lurked underneath it were just dissidents of this philosophy. He clarified to Puss Titter that the check was worthless, a lame come on with no apparent value other than it's melancholic appearance. For it to be cashed, a sum larger than its worth had to be spent on some ridiculous and unwelcome endeavor. No comfortable anagram could have reversed the unwelcome admission that the check was a spurious commodity worth nothing. In the atmosphere of the cubicle, the dust motes hardened with the inaccessible frankness of the unwelcome news and the epic dictate rioted above every surface. Still, the bank draft somehow stimulated last ditch entreaties from Puss Titter, as if there were a mutual vanity between her and the money. But it was all over, like the concluding laughter of a brave man staggering across a zone of dark insistence. She could not accept it. Puss Titter felt the suitable goodness of her moderate game evaporate, and she withdrew her aspirations from the unpredictable circuit like a bitter activist leaving through a hidden door. She mumbled feeble adieus to the rapturous belongings she had already considered hers in perpetuity. Her mystic luxury was now dressed in doom and the unexpected bad news also sank into Baron Ladyship like an unworthy salary.

There was nothing left in the room but the faint schedule of her departure.

The Bodice Ripper waved the check at her as if he was already signaling farewell. As Puss Titter gathered her annoyances she felt like a native enslaved by the uneasy idiom of a foreigner's obscene password. The check wasn't even worth keeping as a memento mori—it was just another crushed article, quibbling unnecessarily before its death. The expanded ingredients of its failure had become yet another list of enlarged nuisances. Puss Titter felt as though an expected disease had finally arrived. Her query had bumped up against the search for an answer and its rounded bite had resulted in an arcane heresy. It was as though a favorite acquaintance had slipped into objectionable laughter, meanwhile steering past any conveniences to reach an accidental conclusion.

The stream of events had averaged the false anticipation across a factual generator; it was time for Puss Titter and Baron Ladyship to shy away from any subsequent malfunctions. The unexpected liberal misfortune had cut the pair like a virtual razor and it seemed that there was no usable relief. They began to migrate towards the door through the forfeited furniture of The Bodice Ripper's domestic confines. Yet even as they made their exeunt, it was impossible to estimate when the sentiments that plagued the two would end. As they closed the door, a rose narrative bowed in the carpet, and from the cabinet an isolated bottle of liquor muttered like a beat token.

The atmospheric hotel had profiled the strange fantasy like a bankrupt disguise contradicting a promise. Once out on the boulevard, Baron Ladyship became terrified of any violent reaction that Puss Titter might have to The Bodice Ripper's heretical declaration. As their walk progressed he began to realize that she had fortunately absorbed the disastrous bulletin with a unifying speed and was already accelerating the bond over her next heated purchase. Her pale haircut had bucked over the incident, but now her manifesto had matured and a new terminology yawned against any substitute.

All around them the prerequisite cityscape commenced a sincere commentary, each cased gesture understood without the aid of an interpreter. Off in the distance a kidnapped observer and his nameless identifier kicked a postponed annoyance, like the workload doom of a lethal assignment. The epic dispute of the streets yawned around them like a supernatural blanket as they turned at the functioning complex near the drained playground.

Baron Ladyship and Puss Titter were not inclined to be cheerful, so neither one of them would admit to speaking. As the travelers stirred down Biblical Road in silence, a rising gateway sighed as a bandwagon and holy carriage left the vicarage, bearing down on them like a butter machine. Every flashing noun compromised the cruise like a fluent resource, but a smaller rave had purged the freeway before the quaint conveyance was able to qualify the stress. Whatever insults the sixth choral mass had inflicted on the simplified nuns sailed past them like a beforehand lifestyle. The erstwhile vicar was directing every confined flute, making sure that the iron whistles merged with the licensed circuitry. A provisional verse marched above the negative perspective as the players joined their concerns throughout the low hassle with the unsung grievances. Puss Titter leaned against Baron Ladyship while the baffling lifestyle passed them, as meaningless as an impartial documentary looking for a positive opinion. Beyond them a spur discriminated against a configured slash and the band reached a stirring coda as it turned off Biblical Road.

The musical riot had broken the spell of quietude so Baron Ladyship began his well considered dictation. He extended his admitted blessings and reaffirmed his doubtful sympathies, finishing his monologue by estimating his motionless sentiments end. There was a tragic look again on Puss Titter's face, as if she were a widow who has suddenly been made irrefutably aware of death but prefers to continue with her rapturous disbelief of the inevitable end. Still, there was no way to make her reasonable opposition succeed against reality's bursting insight, and the comedic pointlessness of the heavy project finally triggered Puss Titter to burst out in the hierarchy of concluding laughter that Baron Ladyship had hoped for since they left The Impervious Hotel. By the time an understandable economy had summarized their unambiguous return to Critter Tightwad's rolled institute, Puss Titter's pulsing closet disappointment was only a symbolic headache.

BROKEN AND SESSILE

The new weekday dashed against the horizon as the sun rose, recovering the contours obliterated by night. The morning light rioted across the lawns as its sky fumed over their superficial rescue, the cooperating landscape summarizing the lenient ritual like a pretend creature. A soiled motorcycle club spun down the main street of Hill Town Eye, passing the spoiled chaos of the circuit towers and their merging extremists. Steaming beneath the misidentified cathedral, a dubious bishop swept the evening's bacterium onto the shoes of an ambitious atheist while in the mess hall of the city jail a prisoner blew smoke at another dissident burglar. Out on the parade grounds of the university campus, a military policeman and an unethical official buttonholed a four star general, a deed that met with cordial sympathies but little action.

As hockey practice began in the park, an amateur gnome negotiated his diagonal against the ice, watching the rival team harden with a dark insistence. At the school a cheerleader pressed against her philosophy teacher, their mutual slang making the team captain jealous of their elaborate chemistry. Overhead, the lead cartoon duck of a rattling flock flew across the distracted climate, disappearing into the atmosphere with a crass noise. In its solo yard a fragile lemon tree staggered a brave shadow across the full fruits of its resignation, bringing forth a reckoning of the day as far spent. A notorious duel commenced inside a garden shed, the soil heaving as a weasel and stray cat malfunctioned in their proper stunt routine.

The sunlight was one of God's successful experiments, guttering its independence against the hierarchy of a practicable geography. Soon the twee gardens beyond the country doors of the saccarine dwellings would give in to the green urgings and explode like a flowering verb, dancing in the wind like a supplementary anecdote.

The alphabetic schedule of the day had begun, kickstarting a sure adventure behind the morning's outrage. Mr. Breakwind glided past a deserted supermarket, half-listening to the gentle musical as a fibrous intern of beggary argued with his cart of jetsam. The speech and epic dictation droned like a commentary despairing into a beat anagram, the street monarch preferring sarcasm to insecurity as he composed a digital dialect. The tirade had a musical style, like a concerto of concluding laughter and bored jazz concerning a swept flood. Somewhere guilty children threatened their jelly, exerting a similar dominion over their objects.

Mr. Breakwind's day had commenced auspiciously enough with a phone call to This Dominique Crushingbore. He had been expecting yet another vocalic silicon disappointment but the telephone had lusted before him and a time had been set at once to share a religious mug of vintage juice at The Chattanooga Codebreak. He headed towards the prevalent coordinates, fingering the blue pill of systematic love and compiling his cozy plan. The worn smiles of the sidewalk surfers forbid any rubbish to creep in underneath Mr. Breakwind's positive crystal impulse as he considered his seduction. In the distance his pornographic objective posed unseen among the reasoning buildings, the architecture's stationary average inspiring a trusting wealth.

An uninteresting downhill yawned before him, the conventional focus somehow bettered by its own blasted flaws. It seemed impossible to Mr. Breakwind that the entire cityscape was ignorant of his mission and concealed anatomy.

He continued past the village pharmacy where a tourist breezed with a continental pulse before the occupied chemistry. On the television behind him a cartoon character recommended the desired explosive as a strong researcher uttered a worried blurb, his grammatical manner confronting the cautionary phenomenon. In any other communal experience a warning rescue would already have been sent, like the tiny molecule that shuts down a feeble giant.

Throughout this scenario muttered a credible sail, its concerned plume pounding any insufficient buffer. As he crossed the street, fiddling across another dirty layer of Hill Town Eye, Mr. Breakwind felt his disregard for Puss Titter railroading through the deserted avenues. The advice that Billy Lucid had given him at the party resonated in his mind like the caring soundtrack of a relaxed nobleman. After all, This Dominique Crushingbore was just a pretty face whereas his wife held the key to a potential million gold teeth. Mr. Breakwind could not act like a pregnant bed rejecting a prophet any longer, he had to start calculating his obligations and hammer the resistance. For the first time in a long while Mr. Breakwind felt guilt interfering with the scandal and his boss heel froze as if he were a captain diverting past a sounded wreck. His pride abided into dread as he neared The Chattanooga Codebreak and he felt like a kid hesitating on the telephone. A troubled sweat cascaded down his face as he felt his unfinished potential rotting in the damp scum of the uninformed landscape.

An incidental truth volunteered itself as Mr. Breakwind's skin elaborated beneath the damaging fuss. Bearing his package like an ambitious liberal expanding above their unemployed stereotype, he entered the frivolous hell of the tavern's chartered space and peered about in the gloom. A pair of piebald aliens stood in the corner booth, authorizing their goodbyes to a spaced out policy wonk from the community dictatorship. A lost taxpayer disappeared into the wrong bathroom, zealously unhitching his belt as he ignored the unpleasant entreaties of the occupants. Two well-built purse maids of terminated principles squatted in a puddle of beer like fertile chickens, pecking at some spilled coins next to a ruptured pocketbook.

Success was not a possession frequently delivered to The Chattanooga Codebreak.

This Dominique Crushingbore sat in her unsure intelligence at the bar, listening to some Mister Estimable cough up his flaccid flirting and perverse signals. A private equilibrium had integrated them like a joint dustbin and they received Mr. Breakwind's approach as if he was a walking death threat. He suddenly felt his entire repetitive anticipations sink beneath the unenthusiastic floor like an ironic bomb. The last thing he needed was a roundabout fuss with some Mister Nun Monkey standing next to his date like a ghost wearing an unpleasant expression. Fortunately, Mr. Breakwind knew from experience that the absolute always emerged from behind a distress, so after postulating the crisp irony of a sarcastic salutation, he began to rave about bigotry, commercial famine and homosexual sports. Occasionally Mr. Breakwind asked his rival repulsive questions, even though he knew his adversary would not be disposed to reply to such incommodious inquiries. Mr. Breakwind hoped that This Dominique Crushingbore would drop the attitude of a competitive flycatcher and let the facts speak in complete phrases for their impudent selves. It would then become obvious that she was wasting time conversing with some Mister Canker Lothario and her full tributary attentions would return to him.

The inclement boyish salaciousness that Mr. Breakwind utilized finally captained the contest and the opponent left, hotly flexing his dyslexic shake pistons.

After this last knot had been tied, the duo breathlessly regarded each other as if looking through a spyglass television. Counting on his psychic arsenal to give him strength, Mr. Breakwind began the evenhanded ruse that he hoped would lead to some quality gossamer stitching and humping with This Dominique Crushingbore. His entertaining advances worked marvelously and, as the debugging flirtation excelled both their expectations, he felt sure that he had fulfilled a major prerequisite for sex. Mr. Breakwind relaxed in his position as the pursuer and eagerly brushed his compliments onto This Dominique Crushingbore, who was apparently relishing her role as the pursued. As his attack incentive gained momentum, Mr. Breakwind utilized his devious charms to persuade the object of his affectations that she would benefit highly from his performance of the famed Bedspring Symphony. As expected, his buzz-saw betrothal beachhead drove her to a hot and nasty extreme so plans were made to finish their premier cocktails and head to the nearest sheet box, most likely the Impervious Hotel.

Crushing her elope breath beneath his balk, This Dominique Crushingbore excused herself and set off for the circumstantial fury breakwater of the powder room. Mr. Breakwind palmed the bitter pill of Viagra into his mouth, downing it with the final dregs of her Cosmopolitiano Gouge as he briefly recollected that it was Puss Titter's favored libation.

The pair departed from the nonsensical calorie bazaar, leaving its mirrored walls to the deputized somersault alcoholics crowding the bar. Mr. Breakwind felt like a native doubling as a dictator as they trekked toward The Impervious Hotel, holding his mobile phone out in front of him like a phone sex divining rod. Meanwhile, This Dominique Crushingbore dictated into her susceptible cell phone, brandishing it like a circulatory gun loaded with a forgotten vocabulary. As he listened to her pedestrian prose, Mr. Breakwind was once again reminded of the noble insight, so often forgotten, that one must suffer for one's art; and, having no art left in his soul, he supposed that he was being tormented for the sins he was about to commit. The undesirable suffix of the surprising mumbo jumbo This Dominique Crushingbore elucidated at top volume began to worry Mr. Breakwind. Their erotic wordplay had ceased once they sailed through the abused exit of the bar and he suddenly felt lost at sea, looking without hope for a deep island. Still, their tryst was about to go live and he and his kind instrument would be field iron ready and no less.

As Mr. Breakwind and This Dominique Crushingbore entered The Impervious Hotel, their arrival rioted above every surface like some sort of deputized somersault aggrandizing their advancement. The lobby of the hotel wore its music loudly, overwhelming the street noise with the absolute perfection of its sincere highlights and burdensome deluge. The brilliant hello

Mr. Breakwind made to the officer at the desk was adulterated by the crisp irony of the sarcastic salutation he received in return: it was apparent they only needed the room for a short-term cataclysm.

As they dangled in the elevator like the incomplete earrings of a boisterous hoodlum, Mr. Breakwind prepared for waging the hypersexual fight that lay before him. Feeling that he owed the situation some enthusiasm, he grabbed This Dominique Crushingbore like a degenerate firework and began whispering rapturous unpleasantries into her admirable ear. It was hardly the diciest serialization of his perversions she had heard but it set her quivering with an internal energy and considerate fire. She confirmed the algebra behind his equation, lighting up like an evolutionary consumer on a binge. No adopted spoof would interfere with the acceleration of her grateful virus, no pointed pitfall could pose a threat to her maximum prosecution.

The doors staggered open with a mediaeval symmetry, rending the elevator's safe harbor like a sabotaged vessel.

The aged infrastructure of their room seemed to regard the remarkable feat of their entry as though the whole tabloid scandal was just another inducible routine. A residue of the previous night's tenant stained the sporty geography of the bed like a dispensable wet blanket, even as This Dominique Crushingbore sat on the blemish and grabbed his cock. She pulled at his belt as if playing with the pieces of a deconstructed and forgotten jigsaw puzzle, purring like an engine vending within a beast. Mr. Breakwind tried to step away but she pulled at his zipper with her teeth, looking up from her padded crouch like a deranged cannibal going after a prime cut. She began an obscene narration, making sexual forecasts and brazen predictions as her fluent interference purged any semblance of romance. The rutting chaos boggled Mr. Breakwind and he flashed on how many times Puss Titter's compelling yawns had stifled his cutting efforts, how often his decimal meat had been denied the doubtless deed. He blew the machinery above the succeeding legend and ripped open This Dominique Crushingbore's support camisole, unlocking her teats like a pair of magnificent convicts. He moved in, loosing a maverick whoop as he blasphemed like a maniacal rebel.

Their incorporate breeding pulsed like the covering thoughts of some donated counterpart, yet a stultifying change of fortune had begun. Mr. Breakwind knew that the moment of magnetic twist had arrived but he felt no radial glow, no unique continuum of lust stimulating his module. A sense of frustration sullied his isolated perspective and disappointment reigned over his impotent censure.

Mr. Breakwind's sex had crashed on the useless Viagra, and no sentient subsidiary could mitigate the outrage based on that erred calculation.

His sexual incompetence was a dulling inadequacy, disappointing This Dominique Crushingbore and her flesh trigger like the simpering of an ineligible fairy. It was apparent to Mr. Breakwind that no amount of steadfast determination could reinstate his perverse relevance and raise his manhood like a phoenix. There was no etymology that he could use to explain away the worthless Viagra and its pall of disaster; it was a private failure he could relate to no one. His passionate icon had become as foul as a misguided nun in a burned universe. The erroneous overhead and precise obstruction of Mr.

Breakwind's defeat alternated with the heritage of his failure; an official observer would have given his tired cookie an operating score of zero.

The heat was set on conflagration as This Dominique Crushingbore loosed her unreserved contempt without hesitation. She leaned scornfully into Mr. Breakwind's chaotic cowardice as she repositioned her dress. There would be none of the insistent pleasures she had been promised and the potential fury of her explosive filter swept around the unstimulating episode

The monstrous secret that had carried Mr. Breakwind along the road of erotic dreams was just a shabby coach of sad impressions trundling past a procession of disinterested temperance ladies. The glorious anti-impotence drug had proven itself to be just another monument to failure, an impatient sexual property infringement that baffled hope. There was no time for philosophic introspections or metaphysical conjectures, all he could do was color his vocabulary with apologies for this noteworthy deviation. The turbulence and anger he felt filled the nursery palace with the unsuitable sunshine of a disaster that could not be undone.

This Dominique Crushingbore regarded Mr. Breakwind as if he were some trademarked dust heap found by the side of a road full of sullen holes. The shabbiness of the lodgings suddenly became overwhelming and she smiled wearily, thrusting his damaged façade away from her face with tremulous hands as she migrated across the wastes of the room. Mr. Breakwind stood broken and sessile in his appointed malfunction, a sorrowful and rhythmic fascination washing across his face as she slogged into the falsetto heat like a halfwit leaving the forest.

LYSERGIC AND DYADIC PURSUITS

A **graffito invitation reared the orchestral touch** to chalk as Puss Titter gained momentum on the way back to her hut after parting company with Baron Ladyship. She marauded through the shrunken streets like a nihilistic middleman lost in thought, ignoring the passing buildings with their roomfuls of hurray emitting newborns and dappled congestive ancients. Her toes curled when she recalled behaving like an unnecessary blunderbuss in the lodgings of The Bodice Ripper, wearing her pacifier outside of the cube like a gabardine baccalaureate as she had waved the ridiculous check in the aether. Puss Titter felt debased, her gumption lost in the miasmal shuffle of the neurofinancial burnout. It wasn't that she expected some histamine salaams for her efforts; after all, her delivered eagerness and exquisite resolve made for no offense. The problem was that the promised money had corrupted her popish anatomy and raised her devious and indisputable hopes for an end to the financial scantiness that plagued her.

On the corner, a prejudiced pool shark wolfed down his dinner as if acting in a sober drama while a dominated worker and greedy policeman postulated tunneling to heaven like a boring counterexample. In the hardy void of the day outside of Puss Titter's interior psychic assault, her effect was minimal. It was time for Puss Titter to realize that if there was one thing she was, she certainly wasn't a deserted baby coward. Her top ten numerals were numbered just one and she counted herself only; even Mr. Breakwind was peripheral to that. She was episodic and exclusionary, like a churchgoing ogress worshipping an ignoramus deity, the discourse insincere or worse.

Puss Titter set out across the park, chafing in the crosslink sling of her editorial harness.

Then, where the mow yawned in full bloom next to the orange trees fruiting with the cats lounging underneath like monseigneurs in debt, Puss Titter spied a choppy fisticuff phenomenon. Alone and ignored by the out-of-bounds feline academes lay an object of primal inspiration and pure conjecture, something that cast a suitable sunshine over the damaged disk of her sad impressions. A small briefcase lay on the grass, its solitude an allusion to some past luxurious failure of attention. Now, it was absolutely fascinating in its plumage of reasons to be there, like a bodiless monument to itself. And, just as a loving pet must decide to cross the road, the roundabout fuss of the find required that she examine the practicable goods.

She hefted up the diminutive baggage with baffled hope, like a ghost lured along gently by an article in the abstract.

To Puss Titter's burst amazement the briefcase was filled with money, the joy green glowing like an operating mythology. She held the treasure like a vapor that quickly passeth away, even in the clearness of her noisy hope the uneasy find didn't seem real. Puss Titter slammed the stumbling container shut before any vulgar sirs could hungrily settle nearby; she would make no sacrifices. Social Darwinism may have conferred Puss Titter magisterial approval on her infringement, but art brought sweet gratitude to her earnest lips.

Puss Titter loped away as the delicate wind that stirred the grass blades seemed to become a whirlwind of elation addressing the pearls that now lay along her course. The racket of her thrilling stunt was like the delightful music of some antisocial classic film pulsing in the skull of a compelled robot. Puss Titter had become a burglar whose only allegiance lay with her fellow moral dissidents. As she made her way to The Chattanooga Codebreak Bar with the satchel stuffed in her jazz pants as though pregnant, a wave of curiosity and guilt washed through her like a relentless mixture.

Mr. Breakwind slammed the door of the hotel room, the paintings kicking against the walls as he entered the coarse channel of his flight. His abysmal level of bedroom ardor with This Dominique Crushingbore made him feel like a ghastly defendant in a garbage can pocket, deserted by his sentinels forever. Even the resultant secret tornado of useless mechanical attempts he had made to resuscitate his manhood for his own edification had failed. He was in no mood for conversation with any one, every bone in his body ached and his head throbbed with a dull pain. Still, these physical discomforts caused him less annoyance than the numerous inconveniences and hardships he had suffered on what he now denominated a fool's errand. He should have taken the dose while with his wife, then his stultifying performance would have been of no importance. Mr. Breakwind had lost his head start and was unlikely to regain it at any further stage of the game.

His disappointing impotence had discarded any covering speculations of significant bliss. As he tottered away from The Impervious Hotel, Mr. Breakwind's shadow followed him with a repulsive delight, mimicking his forlorn gestures like a talented and ethereal lunatic. The bent diary of his day progressed like a sick phenomenon as he beat through the crowded square, the impersonal blood ministers and advisory beeraholics distinctly avoiding the smoldering container of his failure. Even the infallible electorate camped in their futile gear by the library seemed to object to his faked ministrations, their faulty silence worse than the usual entreaties for spare change. The entire burned universe appeared to grow more aged with every flagging effort Mr. Breakwind made on this tiring expedition to The Chattanooga Codebreak Bar for a competent overdose of whisky.

Then, in the supermarket collision of the boulevards, the substance he had taken kicked in like an invaluable gasoline. The tangential strokes of Mr. Breakwind's trouser suit began goading his devil's pole with an insistence so fantastic that it pulsed against his amended excess like the prerequisite hardening of a stone. Every step that he took increased the lyrical radius of his special muscle, making his nasty castle persist as if the dictates of a prostitute had become sacrament. Mr. Breakwind felt his charming hardship stiffening into an intuitive rod as he witnessed every pressing female in the throng; he felt like an erotic researcher at a pornographic event redeeming an assumed award. The blue steel had fixed his bayonet as if he were an errant preacher on a precious staircase above a sermon, doing away with all the theoretical gibberish in order to ease his return to carnality.

The new sexed up incentive hurled Mr. Breakwind out of his fog like a maid drying the linens of an end bed in an astonished apartment. It may have been the renaissance of his hard pink counsel, but as he trod through the kettle divide to the café, Mr. Breakwind felt a rising panic at the pragmatic clash of his situation. He now had a rail below the navel, but no pornographic constituent to suffer his successful violations. Such an energetic modulus required the hooked logic of a radical improvisation. It was time to renew the boisterous stamina of his marriage vows and give his wife and her furry bonnet his two-buttocked cut for a change. Mr. Breakwind's mechanical member was going to bring it on home like a distant monarch hunting with a sordid pointer.

Puss Titter sat in the formaldehyde chaos of The Chattanooga Codebreak Bar, her favored cocktail set up in front of her like an ignored trap. The day's major gossip ingredient was the incontrovertible blessing of her discovery on the grass; but now, after a few Cosmopolitianos, the unexpected honorarium was no longer a novelty. Puss Titter had no clue how to fluctuate with the data so she lounged with a laughing kindness on her face, its horror left in reserve to ward off any unwanted invitations to company.

Now that she had the same famine supplements as the moneyed elite, she could afford to be an incompetent revolutionary and sabotage any of reality's rave defects.

Mr. Breakwind suddenly exploded through the side wicket of the saloon like a year-end god rampaging in the Temple of Moderate Remedies. Rattled by his chosen hardship, he went straight to the bar without registering any of the defrocked ingrates or bullfinch aristocrats on their perpetual pub-crawls. Mr. Breakwind whooped down his whisky then turned to survey his fellow inmates in the public house, expecting to see only dud horseflesh. But when he saw his wife he beamed like a romance bench, his heart reverberating for her breadfruit accommodations as she coruscated a glow of boisterous stamina like a novice nihilist.

Walking towards Puss Titter, Mr. Breakwind allowed his mind to improvise an image of her wearing convincing leather in a bedroom landscape of provoked blankets. He imagined his wife waiting for an artistic intercourse, playing with herself like some famous half breed in the marching band of a sexy army as the rarest prejudice of her sexual apocrypha evaporated in the plagued game of their coupling.

Mr. Breakwind cut through the bar's interference, approaching her exhaustive table as Puss Titter ascended like an intimate philosopher bicycling over retail pornography. Her cardboard comfort overflowed over the lit logic that warmed to the touching premise that she envisioned: her husband's utter fidelity delivered to her like the expensive gifts she would distribute to him. His fantastic insistence and amended excess would orientate his anarchy to the plagued game of their vanity, overlapping any remaining allegorical surplus.

As they kissed, their available mouths thirsted for each other's erotic bitmap.

Both money and sex migrate through each human being without compromise. Sex is a high-staked game, surrounded by an audience of screaming mankind. Mr. Breakwind's mean width pressed against Puss Titter's wealth generator as if her tailored billfold covered the plagued tangents of an unsupported strategy. Both of them had been expecting their own private redemption, waiting for it like a selected metaphor buried in the uninteresting drivel of an anonymous visitor. Puss Titter's money powered the irresistible symptoms, like an editorial appraisal that excludes sex in a coherent suite. They blushed up against each other, lysergic and dyadic in their pursuit of desirous raptures in the justice country of their bedroom.

A BEAUTIFUL
CONTINENT

Night began its bloodshot serenade, falling across the city as if directed by the hand of an unknown driver. Earth had long since gone mean, its hemisphere of darkness slowly obscuring the only view left to the chaos teams that overpopulated Hill Town Eye. The last knot of the day had been tied, and in the academies the lessons had been forgotten.

Critter Tightwad sat in the lobby of his hotel, reveling in the phantom weight of his surroundings as the ill-advised industry types that followed his denuded current began their pointed drinking. The Ivory Negro was considered the cowboy of the moment, but with nothing to do other than emphasize the bellhops he floundered and soon lost that distinction. Up in Critter Tightwad's room, Fez Croon waited like an untoward apprentice, making no attempt to crash in on his rehearsed innovations as he lounged in his scatterbrained enthusiasm and listened to abusive audiotronics.

Across town, Saturnine Hour began at The Chattanooga Codebreak Bar as a puffed matron onstage got the only depressible attention available from a table of corrupt bookies. In the corner booth, Deanna Cuckoo Esplanade and Dunbar Pooh laughed like a ferrite evensong as Baron Ladyship recounted the thunderously spectacular financial improvisations that afternoon in The Bodice Ripper's housing. They grew more ominous and uninhibited, rolling in the profligate information's debut like drunken sycophants.

This Dominique Crushingbore downbeat her way in to The Crash Apache Lounge with a party of bridegrooms and doubt freaks from Anastigmatic Industries. They were mythically scoffed at by the bar flies and other diffeomorphic organisms, their poetic contrariness appearing just a bit too extroverted and unjustifiably burdensome to the regulars. She was prepared to look beyond sociable felicity and sympathize with the insipidity of what she thought was the locals' continuing admiration, but she had wasted a complete hour on the wrong side and there wasn't much left for them to comport themselves with.

Billy Lucid inched home from work through the patterned blood of a predatory windstorm, mulling on the ways that a simple phrase became a hysteron proteron. He drove with a silent look on his face, trying to prove that "black and white" was a leisured observation but "white and black" was an in depth ignorance. In the seat next to him Scintilla Boniface threw him indecipherable deferential looks, as if he were a hydrodynamic baboon. As he idled in the traffic he felt like a Hellenic figure who has been cursed by the murderous wastage of his talents, leaving only a disgruntled stamina to keep him solvent.

As twilight compressed the data of the day's events, the evening's aberrant genesis extended into every vicinity. The night's headline had been "More Dead for More Country", and it was written on the grenade bonnet of the crumbled taxi that carried Mr. Breakwind and Puss Titter through the consonant door opening of their garage and deep into the interior grotto.

Mr. Breakwind winced as he disembarked, the criminal position of his stone pine forcing him to advance as if laying male eggs. The audacious intentions that he had savored during his pilgrimage from The Chattanooga Codebreak Bar now thwarted his progress and he crept forward like a transported ruin. Puss Titter made drunken and muddled attempts to assist her husband while mounting the gradual gateway as his steaming blast condensed around them. They put all their joy miles in solid order, passing the aggregating paintings of important cities before falling into the matrix of their bedroom's journey chamber.

The inconvenient but stimulating confines of the boudoir sabotaged any attempts at decency; the room powered sex.

It was time for Mr. Breakwind to unsheath his starring rod and reveal the power coordinates of its angle. Puss Titter blushed up to him, hastened in her pursuit of his manhood by her wonderment at his handsome command of the stiff extension. For the second time that day Mr. Breakwind's zipper was undone by foreign teeth, and Puss Titter made a low revving sound as she attended to his weapon with her exclusive craft. She watched herself in the mirror, hungering anew as she admired her own pornographic appetite. Mr. Breakwind burst with similar vanity as he blazed under the effects of the stimulant he had ingested.

They looked like scandalized royalty, exiled there in each other's sinful empire.

Puss Titter rose as if gravity was an insufficient proposal, her legs coining a salacious glance from Mr. Breakwind. She made a wild gesture and suddenly the air above them was filled with hundred dollar bills, floating like bits of a chaotic puzzle released from some imposed order. The dreamy room was transformed into an emerald snow globe, cash littering the floor and floating in the ether above the ball bearing and priapic couple. Mr. Breakwind hesitated underneath the poetic shower then ripped open Puss Titter's dress, sucking at her creamy teats like a luxurious food. They leaned into each other, dropping clothes like immodest and unapologetic servants involved in a bedroom sabotage.

Their resolute sex machine pumped underneath the cascade of cash, Puss Titter's socket receiving Mr. Breakwind's ambrosial charge like an effervescent initiate. She bent over as their fulsome concatenation continued, twisting her bandwagon tail to match his sexual mastery and indefatigable arousal.

They separated and Puss Titter drifted across the room like a beautiful continent.

Her amygdaloidal sweetness was juvenile and immediate, exactly what Mr. Breakwind's hooked logic called for. They fell onto the bed, the love cradle's indiscrete mythology buried by an ace chunk of century bills. As he lathered on top of Puss Titter, Mr. Breakwind's opus extended into physics, his romantic virtues dodging past any possible heresies. Their decisive exertions reached a rapturous resolve, culminating with the understanding that each other's needs formed a wonderful symmetry. Puss Titter screamed out with a fantastic insistence and Mr. Breakwind silently came as they orbited each other in a solar wonder.

The colors deadened in the room as their ardor cooled.

They lay together like two murderers at crossing roads, bound together by sin but forced to wander at odds. Mr. Breakwind leaned over the stroke of Puss Titter's dismissive neck and breathed in the ascending cloud of her funk. She was the only girl who knew the true story of his fall and rise, a real arm through arm type, a heavy love-nation flower dancer. Mr. Breakwind imagined that up in the heavens her guardian angel was digging deep in a basket of souls like an old woman looking for a favorite ball of yarn.

Mr. Breakwind's presence took a purely material shape as he picked up a hundred and left the room, walking alone into the regional sanctuaries of their infectious burrow like a human being tailpipe.

ABOUT THE AUTHOR

Opinionated but informed, esthetic and well-traveled, Anthony Ausgang was born on the island of Trinidad in 1959, raised in Texas and is now a Los Angeles resident. Though principally notorious as the world's most hallucinatory low-brow cat painter, he also puts pen to palimpsest, abandoning conventional narrative for abstracted story lines in much the same way as his art discards the human figure in favor of the feline. When not enjoying classic novels and pulp fiction, he admires the beauty in both a Rembrandt and a rat rod.

SOURCE SPAM EXEMPLUM

The hum puzzles! My upstairs flesh assumes the appraisal. Should a universe score with the felt soup? The on effect proceeds before the girl. A pursued wren dashes under the stunning graffito. A hired surname bridges the acquaintance above the mass essence. The back speaks? When will the blood hunt? Past whatever daylight expires the speeding priest. This nick swamps the fallen gut. The suspected percent gangs a bond stack. A pan intelligence barks opposite an alien mythology. A whistle overlaps! Below a horrible smile returns the rhetorical participant. When will a fringe synthesis progress? Whatever familiar rock flashes the device. The game balls the arithmetic fake. When can the starred apparatus prosecute within a supernatural? An incorporating throughput blinks after the organ. The intimate scrap counts next to the historic mortal. The fume scratches the implicit ignorance. Should the must incompetent shy away? Should the ripping manufacturer junk the divine? A programmable capitalist operates any projecting march. An ambiguous word sockets the economy. The offset leaps the bookshop underneath the seven theater. The counter regret fasts across the python. The wealthy drivel fusses near the straw. A reserved propaganda hurts. A glossy attribute gossips before our egg. The second foot hunts. Across the coupled scheme chooses the drying desert. A concern messes with a ridiculous audience. Does a crowd desire the manager? The emotional librarian bays above the smallish pulse. The forty variance contests the tunnel. The idiosyncratic light exits. The meal crafts the author. A misuse rocks against the door! The organ runs? How will a chief advance? His recipient succeeds near a closing horror. The task trashes the faith after the every network. The bean matures beside a reign. A racket spites the intact truth across the refund. Without the irritating outline advertises her smug upgrade. Every guideline combats a tribe. The snow dines. My minimum composer beefs the key smoker. The longer machinery bubbles underneath the loose residence. The young advertises across the logic! A soap surnames an attribute. The craft simulates the late youth around the intelligence. The summer evidence proceeds across the few scheme.

Paper napkin turn signal for short order cooks amorously lunatic likeable curses federal bubble baths toward abstraction and crank case labyrinths pickup truck recliner around about girls somnambulist beyond secretly tornado behind garbage can pocket ski lodge behind tuba player cloud formation around polar bear fruit cake but about scooby snack secretly because debutantes and brides lazily recliner of line dancer orbiting curses cosmopolitan skyscraper.

Erectile dysfunction has become extremely widespread with years of technological break out and daily hustle and bustle of big cities. It is sometimes unthinkable for a modern man to devote himself to some thing other than working almost 24/7, but what are the sad outcomes of this workaholic craze? Weak libido, next to no stamina in bed and inability to meet woman's expectations in moments of intimacy make up the price for being successful in other spheres of your life. This cure is a bomb! What else can make you a love-hero in 15 minutes? What else can make girls worship you and want only you again and again? Only these pilules!

Made in the USA
San Bernardino, CA
19 September 2013